The Dare to Love Series and NY Dares Series

Dare to Love Series

Book 1: *Dare to Love* (Ian & Riley)
Book 2: *Dare to Desire* (Alex & Madison)
Book 3: *Dare to Touch* (Olivia & Dylan)
Book 4: *Dare to Hold* (Scott & Meg)
Book 5: *Dare to Rock* (Avery & Grey)
Book 6: *Dare to Take* (Tyler & Ella)

NY Dares Series

Book 1: *Dare to Surrender* (Gabe & Isabelle)
Book 2: *Dare to Submit* (Decklan & Amanda)
Book 3: *Dare to Seduce* (Max & Lucy)

The NY Dares books are more erotic/hotter books.

Dear Reader,

The NY Dares are the cousins of the Dare to
Love series characters. These three books, *Dare to
Surrender*, *Dare to Submit*, and *Dare to Seduce*, all contain
exceptionally hotter content—including erotic BDSM
elements—while still being emotional Carly Phillips
stories.

Thank you for joining me for the ride, and enjoy!

All the best,
Carly

CONTENTS

Chapter One

*S*he submitted without the comfort he'd expect to see from a woman who'd been coming to this club for over six months. In the main room, members were in all states of dress, some naked, some in leather, all comfortable with themselves. She dropped gracefully to her knees, legs spread wide, palms up, and yet he sensed her discomfort from across the darkened room. The sound of pleasure, of sex, of pain echoed from the play areas nearby. To most, it was familiar, comforting. It should be the same for her, but her posture was too stiff, her entire demeanor, too wary. Possibly because she played with a different man each time. Searching for something. *For what?* Decklan Dare wondered, not that he understood why he cared. But she called to him. Had from the first.

So he watched her. Just as he watched for her arrival, uneasy when too much time passed between her visits. She didn't show up more than once, sometimes twice, a month. He wasn't here much more often but tried to time his visits with what he knew of her past schedule. Ridiculous. She was just another female and not one he'd ever played with, at that. But she was soft and rounded in just the right places, curvy in a way that appealed to him when no one before had ever reached that deep.

He shook his head and told himself to move on. Find some-one else. Someone who knew he had no expectations but for the night. But he no longer used the club for pleasure. He'd tired of it awhile back. He came to relax here with friends, that's all.

His gaze fell back to *her*. She shifted her body uncomfort-ably, and Decklan frowned. He'd always disliked protocol. He'd never expected it. Didn't need it. He'd bet she didn't either. She just needed a man she believed in—that was apparent.

Not him. She looked too vulnerable for someone who took, gave the minimum, and walked away.

"Still fighting it?" his best friend, Max Savage, asked.

Decklan cocked an eyebrow. "Fighting what?" he asked, although it was stupid to play dumb. Max knew him better than he knew himself.

"Yourself. Go play with her. Get it out of your system." Max eased himself onto a barstool beside Decklan. "Better than watching her and wondering. Besides, you need to get laid."

Decklan clenched his fist in his hand. His brother, Gabe, had told him the same thing. "You know as well as I do that I can't give her what she needs."

Max barked out a laugh. "Like you'd even know what that is?"

"I can guess. Does she look like she's found the right guy? She comes here and tries out different men. Obviously she's not into exhibition, because she ends up in one of the private rooms for whatever her kink happens to be, he gets her off, and the next time, she's on to the next guy."

"Sounds perfect for someone who doesn't do relation-ships," Max said, gesturing to the bartender for his regular scotch on the rocks.

The club had a one-drink maximum. Alcohol and con-sensual play didn't go well together. Decklan had already had his, ordered it the minute *she'd* walked in. One look at her curves, the full breasts, perfect indentation at her waist, and that luscious ass he'd like to squeeze, and only a drink would do.

"Or maybe she hasn't found what she needs, and she's looking for a relationship of some kind," Decklan said, guessing at what the beautiful woman was really in search of.

He didn't do those. Had thought neither of the Dare brothers did those. He'd been wrong. Gabe had found Isabelle, and now Deck was left wondering if there was something wrong with him.

Max ran a hand through his longish blond hair. "You could always walk away after."

That was the problem. Decklan was afraid one night with her wouldn't be enough.

He scowled at the scene across the room. She still wasn't comfortable, and Mike, her chosen man of the night, wasn't a patient dom. The monitors had had to intervene more than once in a scene he'd performed, and Decklan watched the duo warily. Maybe that was what she sensed, what made her unable to find her peace.

But in position, her long blonde hair fell over her back. And Decklan's groin tightened at the sight. Every cell in his body rebelled at the notion of the other man's hands on her body, or worse, him thrusting into her wet heat. No doubt that would be the end result. Why else would she choose a private room for play?

"Let Mike fuck her tonight." The bastard now tangled his hands in her hair.

"She doesn't always sleep with the guys she plays with." Max sounded pleased as he imparted the information, then took a long swig of his drink.

"How would you know?" Decklan asked, his shoulders stiffening even more.

The other man shrugged. "I negotiated a scene with her once."

An unexpected wave of jealousy turned Decklan's vision a blurry haze, and he grabbed Max's shirt, only to have the man laugh in his face. "It was before you'd laid eyes on her."

Feeling ridiculous, Decklan released his friend.

"And she wasn't interested in having sex with me." Max smoothed out his shirt, his grin still annoying the shit out of Decklan. "Does that change things for you? Maybe she's not looking for anything but subspace and a couple of orgasms. Surely you can handle giving her that?"

"Fuck you, man."

"Sorry. You're not my type." Max laughed.

Decklan closed his eyes, wondering if the lack of sex with her partners did make a difference. If she just came here to scene and relax, that he could handle. Maybe. But if she wasn't sleeping with someone until she'd established a deeper level of trust, that was beyond his ability to give. But he didn't know how much longer he could go on like this, watching, unable to get her out of his head.

The sound of raised voices caused his eyes to snap open.

Mike stood, and she'd risen to her feet. Her full breasts nearly spilled over the leather corset binding her body with enticing hooks Decklan wanted to open one by one.

Mike said something.

She shook her head.

The dom's face grew hard, and he grabbed her hair.

Her eyes opened wide. "Red." She said the word loud and clear.

Instead of releasing her, Mike yanked her hair harder.

In less than a heartbeat, with Max right behind him, Decklan was out of his chair and heading across the room. He wasn't about to allow a woman to be taken advantage of in his presence. Especially not *this* woman.

"Come on, let me be the first one in this club to get into that pussy." Mike, the dom Amanda had agreed to scene with tonight, pulled her hair harder than she liked, especially when she wasn't near to being aroused by him.

"No." She cringed at the thought. Hadn't they already negotiated? Laid down the accepted rules and boundaries? She'd been uncomfortable all night, and now she knew why her instincts had been on high alert.

"No?" This time he yanked on her hair to show his displeasure. "What about me and my friend?" He spoke louder than was appropriate or necessary, and she blushed as people around them began to look. "One of us in that tight pussy, another in your ass?"

Hell no. "Red!"

"Get your hands off her." This from the man whose dark gaze followed her everywhere but whom she'd never met.

"What's going on here?" John, a club monitor, approached. Fully dressed in leathers and wearing a badge indicating his status, his arrival was exactly what Amanda needed.

He turned a hard and pissed gaze on Mike, the man she'd stupidly opted to play with tonight.

He stepped into her personal space, getting between her and Mike, the asshole. Apparently he had a protective streak.

"The lady said red. Mike didn't respect it. You can take care of the bastard. I've got *her.*"

John nodded, pulling an argumentative Mike away for what looked like a good dressing down.

"Thank you," Amanda said to her rescuer, admiring his take-charge personality, which turned her on as much as his good looks already did. She'd had her eye on him for months.

Cropped, jet-black hair and a strong, chiseled face that knocked her on her ass. He had an air of authority that aroused her.

"My pleasure." He smiled, taking her breath away. Until now, she'd only seen him from across the room. His impact was more potent up close.

She only came to the club once in a while, to try to get what she needed from a guy without the hassle of a relationship. It still amazed her that she'd only ever really desired *him*. But he'd never approached her, and she wasn't the kind of woman to take what she wanted from a man. Never had been. Didn't trust the reaction she'd get in return. There was a reason she had a membership here, where expectations were laid out up front and if someone approached her, he wanted her, if only for the night.

He clearly hadn't.

The deeply ingrained insecurities instilled by her perfection-demanding mother rose to the surface. Too fat. Not pretty enough. Passably smart, but where would that get her?

"Let me take you out of here," he said in a gruff voice, pulling her back to the present. She met his gaze.

The unexpected flare of desire in his dark-blue eyes took her off guard. If he'd approached her earlier or another time, she would have taken him up on the invitation. Now it seemed like he'd made it because he felt sorry for her. She'd been someone's pity fuck once before. Never again. Insecurities were one thing. Being stupid quite another.

"Thank you, but I'm fine."

"No, you're not." He lifted her trembling hand, which made his point for him.

He obviously thought she was upset about the incident with Mike. He was wrong. She was overwhelmed by his masculine scent, and her body trembled with the effort it took not to take him up on the offer. Pheromones didn't care about things like emotions and pity fucks.

"I don't know you," she said, throwing out another, more substantial roadblock.

Even he would understand that after the crap Mike had pulled, not even the security of club membership assured her anyone here was safe. He couldn't expect her to leave with him.

As much as she wanted to.

She shivered, suddenly cold, wishing she were wearing day wear and not this stupid corset and short leather skirt.

"I can vouch for him," Max Savage said. He was a nice guy she'd done a scene with awhile back. He'd relaxed her and taken her close to subspace. Not over. No one took her there. And at the time she'd been with Max, she'd had no interest in sleeping with him.

This guy was another story.

She glanced at Max and tried not to grin. One friend trying to help another get laid. "Nice try, but I don't know you all that well either."

She rubbed her hands up and down the goose bumps on her bare arms.

"What if I told you he was a cop?" Max asked.

"Really?"

He extended his arm, and someone handed him a blanket, which he proceeded to wrap around her shoulders.

"Thank you," she said, immediately feeling better.

"You know me." John, the club monitor who'd hauled Mike away, reappeared by her side. "You can trust Decklan to take care of you. Mike's been warned before. His membership has been revoked."

She blinked in surprise. "I'm glad." The asshole didn't deserve to be in a position of trust.

"Decklan's a decent guy. Don't leave with him if you don't want to, but at least let him get you something cold to drink. You'll feel better, and then you can get changed and leave. I'll walk you out myself," John promised.

Decklan. She tested the name in her head, liking the sound. "A soda sounds good."

The crowd around them had already dispersed, and even Max had walked away, giving his friend a shot on his own.

Good luck, she silently told him. To her way of thinking, they might have passed *I'm interested* looks with their eyes over the last six months, but he hadn't stepped up, which Amanda took personally. Decklan whatever-his-last-name-was would have to bring his A game if he expected her to do any more than drink a soda with him before heading home.

Chapter Two

*A*t work and in his personal life, Decklan laid out the facts and the truth. He didn't tolerate BS or lies. With this woman, who eyed him with an intense amount of distrust coupled with a healthy dose of desire, at least when she thought he wasn't looking, he intended to do the same.

They sat together at the bar. He ordered two club sodas and let her drink in silence, waiting until she was definitely over whatever had happened with Mike. She was. The tense quiet between them now had everything to do with them. She didn't trust him, and his gut said the reasons went deep.

When she put down her drink and met his gaze, he decided it was time.

"I'm Decklan Dare." He held out his hand.

"Amanda Collins." She accepted the gesture, placing her smaller palm against his.

He immediately slid a thumb over the pulse point in her wrist, pleased with the rapid beat that told him she wasn't immune. Just wary.

Wary he could deal with. Now that he was here, he was in for the night.

She attempted to tug her hand back, but he held on tightly, keeping his thumb pressed against her skin. It was his human lie detector, and with this one, he felt sure he'd need it.

"Thank you again for stepping in. Mike was an ass." She bit down on her plump lower lip.

Fuck, he'd like to do the same. He merely nodded in agreement. "I've seen Mike in action before. At least he's gone for good now." He smiled. "So tell me, Amanda, what were you looking for—before your night was so rudely interrupted?"

A rapid increase in her pulse beat in her wrist. He did his best not to grin wider. In the wake of her silence, he decided to cut her some slack. "How about I tell you what I'm looking for instead?"

"I'm listening." She blinked at him, brown eyes wide.

He rested their joined hands on the bar. "I'll start with what I don't want. No protocol. No games. Just hot, sweaty sex," he told her, his cock tenting his dark jeans at the notion of sliding into her tight, wet sheath.

Her eyes darkened with hunger at his honest words. Beneath his thumb, her pulse was racing with the same desire beating inside him. *Good*, he thought—he'd read her correctly. Earlier, he hadn't seen a woman looking to submit; he'd seen a female in need.

And their needs were obviously in sync. "I want you, Amanda. I want to get you out of here and indulge in what I've jerked off to since laying eyes on you months ago. I want my fingers on that gorgeous ass, my cock, burying itself inside you—"

"You had me at 'I want you,'" she said. "There was no need to ruin a good thing with lies." She rose to her feet, ready to bolt.

"I don't like being insulted," he warned, stopping her with his words and stern tone. He narrowed his gaze. "You said you don't know me, so how can you think I'm lying?" He tightened his grip on her hand.

"If you wanted me that much, you would have approached me months ago, and as for my ass, it's too large and—"

"Enough." He changed his mind. Submission was definitely on tonight's agenda. "Are you with me tonight?" he asked her.

She swallowed hard; the delicate lines of her throat moved up and down as she pondered the question. Slowly, she nodded.

He swiveled in his chair and pointed to his lap. "Then lie down. That's ten for calling me a liar. Your ass is spectacular. Lush, round, and made for my hand." He patted his lap again.

No way could she miss the outline of his cock pressing hard and insistent against his pants.

"I don't . . . We didn't negotiate."

"True." He nodded, annoyed that she got inside his head so badly that he forgot the important things. "Is spanking a hard limit?"

"No," she whispered, her eyes dilating at the thought.

"No what?" he asked. "Protocol isn't what I'm looking for." He didn't want to be called sir or master. He did want his name on her perfect lips. Eventually he'd get them on his cock.

"No, Decklan," she said, her voice still soft.

"Exhibition?" he asked.

She glanced nervously around the room. Most people seemed involved in their own play. Max watched from across the bar.

Decklan didn't give a shit.

"It has been. In the past."

He heard a *but* in there and raised an eyebrow.

"But I'm willing to try. With you."

Her breath hitched, and satisfaction soared through him. "Are you wearing underwear?"

A tiny shake of her head. Blood rushed out of his, all of it headed south.

"Then lift that skirt and lie down, or say red and we can both head home. Separately." Everything inside him stilled as he waited. The choice was hers. The power hers. If she walked away, he might not survive it. Another reason he hadn't approached before now.

Eyes wide, her gaze never leaving his, she faced him. Her cheeks flushed a sexy shade of pink. And ever so slowly, she raised her skirt, walked the few steps closer, and thank God, lowered herself over his lap. She shifted, getting comfortable, wriggling against his rock-hard erection, and he groaned aloud.

He glanced down and faced every fantasy he had and then some. Her ass was round and pale, two beautiful globes waiting for his hand. He'd trained at this club, enjoyed it for a time, but had been tempted to leave it for a while now.

But her?

He was nowhere near ready to walk away. He smoothed his hand over one cheek, then the other, her skin butter soft and beckoning. She stiffened at first, but as he caressed her with one hand, she relaxed beneath his touch, and his cock perked up at her easy submission.

"Do you know why you're in this position?" he asked, squeezing her cheek to make sure she was paying attention.

"I said that you lied."

He had to lean closer to hear her. "Your ass is gorgeous," he said, emphasizing his words with his first smack.

"Ouch!" She wriggled beneath him.

"Quiet." He followed the first with two more, one on the other cheek, the third closer to her thigh. The sound and the crack of his hand blended together for him, giving him a rush he hadn't experienced in a while. "I know you don't know me, but you will. I don't lie," he told her, connecting with her flesh. Four. Her ass pinkened beautifully, his marks glowing on her skin.

She no longer made a sound, but her hands clasped his calves through the denim of his jeans, and a moan echoed up toward him. "Your sweet curves were the first thing I noticed about you." Five. His hand stung, and he came down on her once more. This time she arched into his hand, and satisfaction filled him. Six was slightly harder, and he finished up with seven, eight, nine, and ten.

Small whimpers escaped her lips, reaching his ears. This was what he hadn't seen in her before. The total surrender to her feelings. His gut told him there'd be tears in those eyes, not as much from the pain—because he'd gone easy—but from her giving in. She'd earned the release she needed, and he was all too happy to give it to her, despite the fact that he knew once he slid his fingers into her wet heat, he wouldn't be walking away any time soon.

Amanda's ass tingled, and her pussy clenched in desperate need. The minute she'd lain down across Decklan's lap, her head had begun to empty out. Reaching for his legs to anchor herself had felt natural. Right. She deserved the punishment, knowing she'd questioned his words with no good reason behind it except her own insecurities. Her ass was too big, her boobs were too, and so was her stomach. No matter how much she'd dieted in the past, she always had those curves. It was ingrained in her to believe no man would want her.

He claimed otherwise. She needed to believe him. And when the pain transformed into desire, she did. Why else would she bare her ass in front of a room full of people when she never had before? And why did a part of her actually like it? Because it pleased him. That much she understood.

Her sex throbbed, and the more he ran his palm over his handiwork, the more she wanted. Dampness coated her thighs, and she needed to come.

He squeezed her cheeks together, and heat bloomed anew between her thighs, her clit pulsing with desperate need.

"Are you wet, baby?"

"God, yes."

"Let's see." He slid a finger around her pussy, gliding over her wet lips, spreading the cream he'd created. "You're soaking," he said, pure male satisfaction in his tone.

The whimper that escaped barely sounded like her own.

He eased a finger inside her body, and she clenched around him, attempting to grip him tight, hold him in place. But she wasn't running this show. Instead, he pumped that single digit in and out of her channel until she began wriggling against him, seeking deeper contact.

He slapped her again, and she dropped her head on a low moan.

Two fingers thrust deep, and his thumb worked her clit, pressing hard on the tiny nub that controlled her pleasure. In and out, harder and faster until she was writhing uncontrollably against his hand.

"That's a good girl," he said, each plunge of his fingers deeper, that gruff voice sexy enough to cause a mini orgasm on its own.

She lost track of time and place; the only thing that mattered was the collision of her body and his hand. She arched her back, pressing harder against him, reaching for a climax that was so close and so big that her emotions were at the surface. Tears leaked from her eyelids.

And then she exploded on a scream, her orgasm taking over, pulling her up, up, and over. Pleasure like she'd never felt suffusing every cell of her being, and she rode out the wave, rocking on his hand, lost in sensation. And then his digits curled up inside her, hitting a place that was new to her, and tremors started again, this climax harder than the one before.

Just as the waves began subsiding, he pressed on her clit.

"No," she moaned, knowing there was no way her body could take another.

"Yes, you can." He pinched her hard, and she came once more.

It had been ages since Decklan had done aftercare. Yet he sat on a couch in a corner of the club, an out-of-it Amanda wrapped in a blanket, curled in his lap. His cock throbbed with unslaked need, and he welcomed the feeling. It reminded him that there were times when it was worth the sacrifice to hold out. *She'd* reminded him.

"Well, I'll be damned." Max chose a seat beside him and eyed the feminine bundle in his arms, a satisfied smile on his face. "You gave in and you liked it."

"She needed it," Decklan muttered, not wanting to disturb her until she came around on her own. Damn woman thought she was too curvy? Too big? She'd deserved to have that ass slapped. Next time he wanted to bite. To mark her and gain the satisfaction of seeing his imprint on her skin.

He shifted uncomfortably, knowing he couldn't allow himself to get that involved with her. To do so meant some kind of relationship, which in turn involved allowing himself to get close and potentially care. Or even love. Which meant to risk loss. And loss was something Decklan didn't deal well with. He'd lost his parents at nineteen, and he never wanted to feel that kind of pain and out-of-control panic again.

He shook his head to rid himself of the thought before he traveled to that dark place, but the memory didn't negate the fact that he wanted more with this particular woman. More time to figure out why she got to him and more time than he'd had so far.

The bundle in his arms suddenly stirred. He shot Max a pointed look, and the other man rose to his feet. "I'm going. We can pick this up another time."

Or not, Decklan thought irritably. Max liked to psychoanalyze. Decklan didn't.

"What happened?" She glanced around, her big eyes blinking as she came to—and remembered. "Oh. Wow. I never go under like that."

He grinned, unable to help the ridiculous feeling of pride that he'd been able to take her there. "You did. Here, take a drink." He handed her a bottle of water that had been left for her. He unscrewed the cap and held the bottle for her to sip.

She drank some. "Thank you."

"You're welcome." He paused, then decided to push her a little. A woman who looked like her didn't need to suffer from self-esteem issues. "You need to look in a different mirror," he said, tightening his arms so she couldn't bolt.

And she tried to. He held on. "We don't know each other, and I'm not going to push you to talk if you don't want to. Just know I meant what I said."

"Then you're also saying you're shy? That's why it took six months and another guy being an ass in order for you to make a move?"

Shit. So there really was more to her disbelief and calling him a liar earlier. "Are you questioning me again? Because I'm more than happy to add another ten."

She bit down on that full bottom lip. "I'm just being honest. I thought that was part of what went on here." Once again, she tried to push away.

"You tempted me too much," he said, admitting the truth. It was that or giving her up for the night—and that wasn't happening.

As she accepted his answer, the tension eased, and she curled back into him. He released a long breath, unwilling to question it too hard.

He brushed his hand down her long hair, breathing in the mixture of her scent, peaches and arousal. Desire, thick and heavy, kicked him in the groin. She pulled at emotions inside him he'd locked down years ago.

Time to lay out the parameters. "I don't do relationships."

"Me neither."

A waste, he immediately thought. This woman deserved to have a man take care of her. *He* wanted to take care of her.

He immediately discarded the dangerous desire. "Well then, I think we have something in common, and we can go on with our night. Is that what you want?" he asked.

She slowly nodded. "I want that very much, Decklan. I want you."

Chapter Three

*A*manda stepped into the ladies' room to make a phone call, not wanting Decklan to overhear. "You're sure?" she asked, talking into her cell phone.

"They don't call me a computer genius for no reason. I dug deep. Decklan's a decent enough guy. Not a serial killer, no arrests in his past. Nothing hidden either. I'd have found it."

And he would have. Brad Ritter, her boss and very best friend, could hack with the best. She trusted his findings.

"Okay then. I'm not coming back tonight."

"You have the jet fueled for when you're ready. You spend way too much of your life catering to my needs. I'm glad you're taking time for you."

She thought of Decklan's big hands caressing her long-deprived body and sighed happily. "Me too. But don't worry. It's still one night only. It'll just last a little longer, that's all. I'll keep it impersonal and leave in the morning."

"You know I appreciate that you let my father believe we're together."

Amanda glanced at the painted ceiling. Even the bathrooms in this club were first class. She sighed. "It's fine. It's a win-win for us both. I'm happy with my life the way it is, and you and Keith can stay under the radar." Or in the closet, as the case might be.

As right-wing Tea Party Senator Stephan Ritter's son, Brad felt he could never come out and admit his sexual orientation without destroying his father's career. And though Amanda had thankfully put her bulimic past behind her, she wasn't all that trusting of men and relationships. It was simpler to get what she needed sexually at this exclusive club. Brad, her tech geek billionaire best friend, paid for her membership. As she'd said, win-win.

"Well, when you get home tomorrow, I want to hear all about the guy who got you to extend your *couple of hours and only at the club* rule."

No, he would not. What happened in New York would stay in New York. Including how very attracted she was to Decklan and how much she wished she had the normal ability to trust and indulge in relationships. Not that it mattered. Decklan didn't do relationships either.

"I love you for caring. Now I've got to go. I'll see you tomorrow."

"Love you too. Take care and have fun."

She shut her phone and reentered the club to find Decklan, arms folded across his chest, waiting right outside the hallway. "I thought maybe you found a window through which to escape."

"Not a chance." Now that she was in, she was going to enjoy. "I just needed to freshen up and call a friend. Otherwise the cavalry might arrive if I didn't get home on time."

"Good to know someone has your back."

She smiled. "Never doubt it." If she needed anything, Brad would drop everything. They'd been best friends since bonding in college, and nothing could change that. Now she was his personal assistant, allowing him to focus on code while she kept the rest of his life running smoothly.

Decklan placed a hand against the small of her back, a possessive gesture that had her trembling.

"My place or yours?" he asked.

"I'm in from out of town." Brad had two apartments, leased and hidden under fake names, where they stayed when in town for business. One for him, the other for her. They were far from the ultrawealthy area where people would expect Senator Ritter's son to stay and kept both him and Keith protected. She didn't want to take Decklan there and raise questions.

He blinked at the revelation. "Actually, that makes sense. It explains why you're not here more often."

It was her turn to be surprised. "You really did pay attention?"

"Are we back to whether or not I tell the truth?" he asked in a warning tone.

Her ass still ached from his first punishment, and she wanted to move on to the next part of the night. "No, we're good."

"So my place is okay?" he asked.

She nodded.

"I'm just outside of Manhattan. Great Neck," he said.

"I'm okay with that." She could always call a cab if she needed to escape.

"Are you hungry?" he asked.

She shrugged. "I suppose." She'd eaten dinner, but it was getting late, and she could use something to boost her blood sugar. "Are you hungry?"

His eyes darkened. His thumb suddenly pressed against her bottom lip. She sighed, her tongue darting out and licking his salty skin. "Make no mistake, baby. I plan to eat you."

Her breath left in a whoosh. "Oh."

He slid his finger back and forth across her lip. Her nipples puckered at the simple touch, and she felt the pull directly in the apex of her sex.

"You sound like a New Yorker," she said, trying to find a semblance of sanity.

He nodded. "Born and raised. You?"

"Maryland," she murmured, her gaze never leaving his. Those almost-navy eyes mesmerized her, making her feel like she could drown in their depths.

"And where do you live today?" he asked.

"Washington, DC." She pulled herself out of the spell he wove around her, reminding herself she had someone else's secrets to protect even more than her own.

A one-night stand didn't need intimate, get-to-know-you time. But she wanted to learn more about him, and that was a dangerous proposition.

"Are you going to talk all night?" she asked playfully, a tactic to move things along. "Or do you have some moves you want to show me?"

He laughed. "You can be fun," he said, clearly surprised.

She grinned. "I have my moments." With the seriousness of Mike behind her, her insulting herself and that punishment over, she was ready to play.

John, the monitor, winked at her as Decklan led her out and onto the street. With Brad's check, the club staff knowing who she was with, and understanding that Decklan had been vetted and Mike an aberration, Amanda felt safe leaving with him.

He kept his hand protectively on her back as he led her to the lot where he'd parked his car and held open the door for her once the attendant brought the black SUV around. The radio played Top 100, and she settled into the comfortable seat.

"You okay?" he asked.

She nodded. "I am. Thanks." Surprisingly, she was fine. No, she wasn't a woman who normally left a club or bar with a stranger, but Decklan Dare didn't feel like someone she'd never met. And she really wanted one night with this dominant, sexy man.

The rest of the car ride passed in comfortable silence. He didn't push for conversation, and she was still feeling tingly and relaxed from actually reaching subspace with Decklan. Soon he turned off the highway, and after driving through side streets with small homes that were close together, he turned into an apartment complex and parked in a spot out front.

The lot was well lit, enabling her to see that the grounds were well maintained and the building fairly new. Nice but not excessive. Yet membership in the club was a fortune. She couldn't have afforded it if Brad hadn't insisted on making it a perk of her job. She wondered how Mr. Decklan Dare could be a cop who lived here yet be able to afford the membership. Though Brad could get her all the information she wanted on Decklan, she'd never go that far. Safety was one thing, digging and being intrusive another. This was a one-night stand, and her curiosity wouldn't be assuaged any time soon.

Inside the apartment, she found purely masculine decor with a definite flair. A navy, white, and taupe color scheme, comfortable couches, large-screen television.

"Who decorated?" she asked, certain he wasn't the type to hang ornate mirrors or purchase knickknacks to give the place a homier feel.

"My sister, Lucy."

She nodded. "She has good taste."

"It's what she does. My brother, Gabe, runs the family business, which includes exclusive clubs around the country. Ever hear of Elite?"

She nodded, impressed. "I recently read about the opening on the island, Eden."

"That's them. Lucy does the decor."

"A family business, yet you're a cop." She grinned. "Like to do things your way?"

He laughed. "More like that's how Gabe likes to do things. My parents died in an accident when I was nineteen. Gabe took over and made sure I went to college and became a cop because that's all I ever wanted to do. He sacrificed his needs to let me and Lucy have our own."

"I'm sorry," she murmured.

Decklan didn't reply. Sympathy always made him uncomfortable. So did the knowledge that he always felt like he owed Gabe. Another reason he felt so out of control after his parents died. He might have achieved his dream of being in law enforcement, but he'd done it at his big brother's expense. Gabe never complained. But he'd never had a choice in what he wanted to do. Gabe had become the de facto parent. It was one of the reasons Decklan gravitated toward the BDSM scene. Regaining control helped him deal with his darker emotions.

"He sounds like a great guy," Amanda said.

"He's an ass."

Amanda spun to face him, her eyes wide in surprise.

Decklan shrugged. "He is. To everyone but me, Lucy, and his new wife, Isabelle. He had to be to get where he is today. But I respect him even when I want to throttle him."

"I wish I had siblings."

"Only child?"

She shrugged. "Unfortunately."

He was suddenly aware of how intimate the conversation had become. More like two people getting to know one another than the reality—two people who'd come together for sex. He pushed aside the feeling that talking to her was easy and that he wanted to dig deeper into who she was. What had created the insecurities he'd witnessed earlier. The sadness he heard in her tone now.

Time to move the conversation forward. "Come." He directed her into his small kitchen. "Can I get you something to drink?"

She shook her head. "This kitchen is so comfortable. Do you cook?" she asked, glancing around.

"No. I usually pick something up on the way home from work. What about you?"

"I'm an expert."

He turned her to face him, his hand beneath her chin. "If you lived in town, I'd have to have you show me your talents." He was surprised to find he meant it.

She batted her eyelashes at him and said, "If I lived here, I just might do that."

Cute, he thought. She was cute. "Did you eat dinner?" he asked.

"Yes, before the club."

"Good." He stepped closer. Her scent enveloped him. The memory of her warm and wet around his fingers brought him back to instant hardness. "Then we're both ready for *dessert.*"

Her soft lips parted, but no sound came out.

Pleased with her response, he headed to the refrigerator and paused, turning to face her. He had a plan, and now was the time to execute. "In my bedroom now. Down the hall, first door on the right. Clothes off and wait for me there."

Just like that, Decklan was back to being the demanding man from the club. Just like that, Amanda was wet and wanting. Knowing what awaited her if she hesitated, she found herself tempted to wait. But sensing something even better would come her way if she obeyed, she met his hot gaze, nodded, and walked off toward the bedroom.

Nerves beat at her with heavy wings. Old insecurities threatened. At the club, she always negotiated in dim light, then she and her partner engaged in consensual play, bondage and submission, something she'd learned fed the need to please that lived deep inside her. Growing up, she'd always fallen short no matter how hard she tried, be it in schoolwork, sports, or most especially, her looks.

When Brad had suggested she try a BDSM club for her issues, she'd been wary. But she'd discovered he was right. In submission, she'd not only learned to accept herself, something that was obviously still in progress, but also gained the satisfaction of pleasing someone else. And she really wanted to please Decklan, though she intended to keep the lights low here too. She'd desired him from first glance, and he made her want everything she could get from this one night.

With shaking hands, she stripped off her clothes, folded them, and placed them on the dresser. Cool air conditioning embraced her naked body, and she immediately glanced down at her thighs.

A clatter sounded from the kitchen, and she jumped in surprise. The noise reminded her she didn't have much time. *Remember Decklan wants you here.* It was the last thought that gave her the final boost of courage to climb onto his king-sized bed, ease her bare self back against the pillows, and settle in. *But not before dimming the lights.*

She didn't have to wait long. He strode into the bedroom with a bowl of ice cream, spoons, a bottle of chocolate syrup, and a sexy gleam in his eyes that caused her stomach to flip with excitement.

He turned his gaze on her naked body. She knew better than to think the lack of lighting affected his ability to see, except in her mind. Only pride and the lessons learned tonight had her remaining in place.

"I thought I was dessert?" she said, eyeing the items he placed on the nightstand. She couldn't explain the impulse or comfort level that allowed her to tease him while she was so exposed.

He rewarded her with a low growl of clear pleasure. "Oh, baby, you are." He crawled onto the bed, his big body levering up and over hers.

Before she understood his plan, he pulled a Velcro strap hanging from the headboard slat and clasped a cuff over her wrist.

"Remember your safe words. Red, I stop. Yellow, we talk. Green, and we keep going," he said as he did the same to her other hand, binding her to his bedframe. "Now you look good enough to eat."

His approval slid through her like warm honey, and her nipples puckered in response.

"How do you feel?" he asked.

"Green," she murmured, her body trembling. For the second time that night—or maybe ever—her mind began to slip away.

"Should I bind your legs?" he asked, immediately shaking his head, answering his own question. "No. I think I'd like to feel them wrapped around my waist while I sink deep into your pussy."

Her stomach dipped in anticipation.

Decklan slid a hand over her stomach and deliberately paused there. She stiffened reflexively. He felt it as well as saw the flash of panic cross her face.

He continued to watch her, had been since walking into the room and noticing the lack of lights. Not for the first time, he wondered what had put such issues in her head but knew now would be the wrong time to ask. He had to soften her mind, calm her racing thoughts.

Make her believe the truth, that all he wanted was *her*. She was fucking gorgeous, bound to his bed, blonde hair spilling over his sheets. She was all woman, and whoever had convinced her otherwise needed to have his ass kicked.

He kept his palm on the softness of her belly. "I can't wait to feel you clasp me tight inside you and cushion me with those gorgeous curves." At his words, his cock pulsed against his jeans, demanding freedom. "Is that what you want too?"

She nodded, her eyes dilated with the same need riding him.

"Then you need to let me turn on the lights. I want to see all of you."

She swallowed hard, her eyes wide. This was a defining moment. She'd stay or she'd say red. Everything inside him rebelled at the possibility of losing her before he'd really had her.

"Lights?" he asked, easing off the bed and stepping closer to the panel on the wall.

A small nod.

"Then I need to hear you say it."

She narrowed her gaze, and he appreciated the spunk he saw there.

"You can turn on the lights," she said at last. He didn't miss the wariness in her tone.

But he grinned. She had her issues—who didn't?—but she had backbone, and he liked that about her.

"You won't regret it." He hit the switch and turned on the overheads, dimming them for mood but keeping the glow that would enable him to see her creamy skin. "You're fucking perfect."

She opened her mouth, probably to argue, and immediately closed it again. He liked a quick learner, not that he'd mind more punishment. His hand tingled at the thought, and his cock throbbed in agreement. He found it disconcerting to know he'd rather have her trust than the pleasure he found in the control of punishment.

He walked toward the bed and eased down beside her, gratified at the small inhale of breath as he leaned in close and smelled the sexy scent of her arousal.

One hand in her hair, he slid his lips along her jawline, inhaling her intoxicating light perfume, trailed a path down her neck, and settled in to nibble near her collarbone. He tasted the slightly salty tang of her skin before skimming his other hand up her side, cupping one beautifully full breast in his hand.

He ran a thumb over her nipple, feeling it peak even more beneath his touch. "Hungry?" he asked, massaging and tweaking the bud between two fingers.

"Starved," she said, the word a drawn-out moan as she writhed on the bed, her hands pulling at the bindings he wouldn't release.

"Then we should eat. But I wouldn't want to ruin my clothes."

Releasing her breast, he stood and began to undress, aware of her heated gaze watching him with definite approval as he pulled off his shirt. Reaching for the button on his jeans, he eased the zipper down over his straining, aching erection.

She watched, eyes wide and dilated, mouth parted, and he found it damned arousing, especially when a soft moan escaped from the back of her throat.

"You see? Having the lights on isn't just for me." He reached down and took his cock in hand, pumping from base to head in long strokes.

Her eyes widened even more. "You're a tease, Decklan Dare."

He hadn't been, before her. "You bring that out in me."

A pleased smile lifted her lips.

He settled in beside her and picked up the bowl of ice cream. "Now we eat."

Chapter Four

*A*manda couldn't say she'd had a man feed her before, never mind in bed while she was bound, but that's what Decklan did.

He held out a spoonful for her to taste. "Open."

She did as he asked and was rewarded with the most delicious cold treat on her tongue. There was something decadent about being tied up and taken care of. Something freeing. She wasn't even focused on her body anymore. The hot look in his eyes had all but taken care of that.

"Oreo?" she asked, running her tongue along her lips.

His indigo gaze followed the movement. "Cookies and cream." He fed her another bite.

"Mmm."

"Good, huh?"

"You should try some," she said.

A wicked gleam entered his eyes. "I think I will."

Using his finger, he scooped up a dollop of the treat and traced a circle around her breasts, pausing to refresh the ice cream as he worked.

The coldness on her skin provided a delicious contrast with the fire inside her and the heat he generated with his large body alongside hers. He bracketed her on one side, captured her with his sensual assault on her body, lapping up the treat with slick licks of his tongue.

"Mmm." Her nipples puckered and her clit throbbed, need piercing through her.

"Easy, baby. We're just starting." He reached for the chocolate syrup and drizzled it around her breasts and over her nipples.

She arched off the bed, writhing, her body seeking more, more, more. "Decklan, please."

"Please what?" He leaned in, nuzzling her neck, nibbling her skin everywhere but where she needed his touch the most. "Tell me what you want," he said in a dangerous voice.

She *wanted* his mouth on her nipples, desperately needed to feel him bite down and tug so hard that she felt the pull deep in her sex. And she wanted his wicked tongue on her clit next.

But ask for those things? "I can't."

He gripped her chin and turned her face toward him. "You can. I'm not a mind reader, and if you want me to please you, you need to ask for what you want."

She swiped her tongue over her lips and drew a deep breath. This was hard. But disappointing him wasn't an option. Closing her eyes, she whispered, "Taste my nipples."

"Ask me again. And look at me when you do."

He was a tough taskmaster, but he wasn't asking for anything he didn't want to give. He just wanted her trust.

She swallowed hard. Forced her heavy eyelids open. "Lick my nipples."

He leaned down and licked her lightly, first one, then the other, the light whisper coming nowhere even close to what her body craved.

"See? All you have to do is ask. Trust me with your desires, and believe that I'll give you what you need." His gorgeous eyes darkened with his words, his words giving her the courage to give voice to her needs.

Arousal, urgency, and his implied promise made her brave. "Bite down. Suck harder. First my nipples, then I want you to . . ." She hesitated.

"Say it," he commanded, his voice harsh and demanding.

She could do this. Had to or she wouldn't get what she needed, and she needed him, his buff body and his erection pulsing against her hip. He was big and thick, and she shivered at the prospect of taking him inside her. Creamy desire coated her thighs.

He leaned over, his dark hair a heady contrast to her paler skin, and without warning, he bit down on one nipple. She moaned, the sharp sting of pain quickly morphing into pleasure. "Fuck me," she cried out, arching her hips and begging him with her body.

"That I can do."

He pushed up and levered over her, arms muscular, abs defined, and as she'd seen when he undressed, the cut leading down to his groin mouthwatering. Clearly the man worked out. And he smelled as good as he looked, everything inside her melting for him.

He dipped his head, cupped her breasts, and pushed the twin mounds together. She thanked God he hadn't tied her legs, because she squeezed them tight, finding what little relief she could from the pulsating need. Without warning, he sucked one nipple into his mouth, running his tongue around the distended peak before tugging with his teeth, long and hard.

She tipped her head back and moaned, pulling at the restraints that bound her, the mixture of pleasure and pain arousing her beyond reason. He didn't let up, licking, teasing, biting first one nipple then the other, pausing only to give the same treatment to the sensitive skin on and around each breast. With every tweak of a taut bud, her sex pulsed and throbbed.

She writhed beneath him, the sounds coming from her throat foreign to her own ears. "Decklan, please. Please, please, please." Clearly she wasn't above begging.

He reached over, yanked open a nightstand drawer, and pulled out a condom, opening the packet and sliding it on with shaking hands.

She reveled in the fact that she could bring this big man to the brink, wished she could wrap her arms around him, feel the corded muscles in his forearms and back. As aroused as she was by being bound, the desire to stroke and caress him was stronger.

He slid one finger between the creamy folds of her sex. "You ready to take me, baby?"

"Yes," she said, the word coming out in a hiss. Her pussy clenched, an unsuccessful attempt to pull his finger inside her.

He was teasing her, tormenting her, and she couldn't take it. "I want to feel you." She pulled against the restraints. "Untie me, please."

His eyes grew hooded at the request, but she wasn't deterred, nor was she above begging.

"I need to stroke you, to touch you, to hold your cock in my hand."

Decklan hung his head and groaned. Damn, but he was tempted to do as she asked. Tempted for the first time ever. Other women had asked him to release them, but none pulled at his emotions. None made him want the same thing, *her* hands on his body, *her* fingers stroking his cock. He normally needed the women he slept with restrained and under his control. But if Decklan knew one thing, it was that if she wrapped those arms around him and pulled him in emotionally, he was a goner.

He held back, unable to give in, not even for this one woman who made him want with a ferocity that was foreign to him. He didn't miss the irony. He'd pushed her boundaries, and she gave. She pushed his, and he withdrew like a fucking coward.

"I . . . *can't*," he said and hoped she understood how deeply he meant it.

Silence punctuated the next few seconds, and once again, he wondered if she'd use her safe word and walk away. His heart hammered painfully in his chest, begging him to give in and warring with his mind that told him to lock down his emotions.

She ran one leg up and down his calf, touching him the only way she could. "Okay, but you'd better hurry up and fuck me," she said lightly. A request he already knew wasn't easy for her to make once, let alone a second time.

He breathed out a groan of relief. Yet with her acceptance, something warm and tangible passed between them. Something he didn't want to examine too closely. He already knew she threatened his well-erected walls. He was just now learning how dangerous she would be.

He shook his head and refocused his attention. Gripped his cock in one hand and ran the length over the distended pearl of desire beckoning him. Back and forth, he teased her clit until her entire body trembled beneath him. Her arousal coated his erection, and suddenly he couldn't wait another second.

He lined himself up at her entrance and pushed inside. She was as hot as he'd imagined, as wet as he'd made her, and so fucking tight that he didn't know how he'd make it all the way into her without exploding.

"Oh God, Decklan, you feel so good. So big."

He laughed. Actually laughed while thrusting the rest of the way in. "And you're so tight, I could come right now."

"Don't you dare," she muttered. "Not yet." She clamped her inner walls around him, deliberately, if he had to guess.

He knew he was right when she met his gaze and grinned.

"Damn, woman." She wasn't just hot and luscious—she was fun. When did he have fun with women? Fun during sex? "You can be damned sure you're going to come before I do."

"I'd better."

He leaned down and sealed his lips over hers, really kissing her for the first time. Another thing he didn't normally do, because it implied an intimacy he refused to feel.

Until now.

He thrust his tongue inside her waiting mouth. She tasted like cookies and cream and a slice of heaven, and his heart beat harder in his chest when she rubbed her tongue against his. Of its own accord, his body began to move, his hips rolling against hers, his mouth swallowing her groan of pleasure.

Then he took serious control. Hands braced on either side of her, he raised himself up and pulled his cock out, feeling the drag of her inner walls against his hard length before plunging back deep into her wet core.

God, he'd never felt anything like her before. What made her different, he didn't know. And when his body demanded more, he stopped caring.

He picked up a demanding pace, and she met him thrust for thrust, her hips arching, her body accepting all of him as he pounded into her. He ripped his mouth from hers, gasping for breath, only to be greeted by frantic sighs and moans.

"Yes. Harder, please, harder," she insisted.

Her sweet plea mixed with his rising desire. Sweat formed on his forehead, his balls drew up, his climax threatening to barrel into him when suddenly her back arched and she spasmed around him, her own orgasm hitting hard.

"Oh God, Decklan, yes!" she screamed.

His name had him slamming into her again and again, wanting to prolong her pleasure. Tremors shook her far longer than he thought possible, and he struggled to hold back his release. He lost the battle, coming inside her, spilling everything he had to give and more as mini climaxes shuddered through her. Finally, he collapsed against her soft, lush body, completely spent, aware of her breath in his ear.

As soon as he was able, he pushed off her, immediately undid the bindings holding her in place, and scooped her into his arms. He eased her back against the pillows, and she immediately curled into him. Still, he gently massaged her back, arms, and shoulders until he felt certain she'd feel no lingering effects from being tied up.

A little while later, he carried her into the bathroom and turned on the shower, washing the stickiness off them while arousing her body all over again. He towel dried her first, finished up after, and together they collapsed back into bed.

He knew when she fell asleep. Normally he'd get up, pour himself a drink, and wait until he could wake the woman in his bed and make sure she either left or he took her home. *Normally* seemed a long time ago.

For one thing, he hadn't brought a woman here in a while, the restraints unused behind the headboard. No one had appealed to him.

He knew now he'd been waiting for her.

He didn't know what the hell to do about the impact she'd had on him, but he couldn't let it change anything. The fear that lived within him, the petrifying thought of ever experiencing loss and uncertainty again, had him keeping himself apart.

Hours later, the sun streamed into his bedroom. He awoke to a startling realization. He might have fallen asleep with Amanda snuggled against him, but he'd woken up alone.

Chapter Five

*A*manda glanced around Brad's office Monday morning, wondering how he'd managed to make such a mess in the span of one weekend. Although she ought to be used to his method of madness, she was always amazed that he worked in such chaos. She picked up the empty Starbucks cups littering his desk along with the rest of the barely visible surfaces and tossed them in the trash.

"You know the cleaning help will do that." Brad walked into the room, looking every inch the adorable geek and not the billionaire software mogul he actually was.

His dark hair fell over his forehead, the need for a haircut long past bothering. Ripped jeans and a *Star Wars* T-shirt completed his daily look.

She glanced up and smiled. "Yes, but this way you can have clean space to start over and reclutter sooner."

"What would I do without my favorite personal assistant and best friend?" he asked.

"Star in the next episode of *Hoarders*, probably."

"You do keep me sane."

She laughed. "I aim to please."

"Speaking of pleasing . . ." He walked over and pulled the papers she'd begun to straighten out of her hands. "It's been over a month. When are you going to go back to the club?"

She stiffened. Until now, Brad had respected her moratorium on the subject of New York. Because she didn't want to talk about *him*.

"I can't go back," she said, pushing memories of Decklan out of her mind the way she did anytime she had a free moment of thought.

"And you haven't told me why."

She typically told him everything that went on in her life. That's what best friends were for. Gay best friends were even better, since there were no messy hormones or potential hurt feelings ever involved. But ever since she'd snuck out on Decklan over a month ago, she'd been eaten up by guilt, flooded by memories of that night, and yes, consumed with desire for the man she'd left behind.

But worse than all those things combined was the vision that wouldn't leave her, of the haunted look in Decklan's eyes when she'd asked him to release her hands. As a result of the pain she sensed lived inside him, she'd been all too eager to let him have his way. She, of all people, understood limits and emotional hurt.

Obviously he bound women for a reason. Something was eating away at him, and she desperately wanted to be the one to help him overcome it. *Stupid, stupid, stupid.* She had her own issues that plagued her and another man's life in her hands. Brad had been the best friend she'd ever had, the family she'd created, and without him, she might not be the woman she was today.

She couldn't leave him vulnerable to his father's inner circle of vultures and the special-interest groups that funded him. If Brad were outed, dangerous people would be very angry. She wouldn't abandon him just because she couldn't forget a sexy man who'd touched her body and her soul one fateful night.

"Earth to Amanda." Brad's hand came down on her shoulder.

She jumped at the unexpected contact, her heart racing in her chest.

"Sorry. Where were you?" he asked her, concern in his tone.

"Nowhere important." She turned to him with her sunniest smile. "Now can we get down to business?"

He eyed her with frustration in his dark eyes. "Amanda—"

"No. I don't want to talk about it." To make her point, she picked up another stack of haphazardly piled papers.

"I did some further digging . . ." Brad said.

Her eyes opened wide, and anger immediately surfaced. "How could you? It was one thing to look into Decklan to make sure I was safe. Another to do it for kicks." She clenched the papers in her hands so hard that they crinkled irreparably.

"Do you really think I get my kicks seeing you miserable?" He both looked and sounded hurt at the thought. "I know how much you want to see this guy again. I figure eventually you will. That being the case, I needed to know more than he's a decent guy with no serial killers in his family history." He grinned in an attempt to soften her up. "Come on. You'd do the same for me. If you had my hacking skills, that is."

She rolled her eyes. He was sweet and meant well, but she was still upset with him. "Don't tell me what you found out." If she learned anything about Decklan, it would be from him and no other way.

He raised both hands in a gesture of defeat. "Suit yourself."

That was the problem. If she suited herself, she'd be back in New York, looking to find Decklan at the club.

Decklan sat at the club, nursing a drink and, yes, dammit, brooding. He had access to an entire police department database, giving him the ability to look into one Ms. Amanda Collins if he wanted to. But why bother with a woman only too happy to slip out of his bed and disappear on him for over a month?

Some would say the fact that he couldn't get her soft moans and cries of ecstasy out of his head was reason enough. In Decklan's mind, that only meant she threatened the stability he'd created in his life and the control that kept him sane. Which didn't mean he wasn't a staple at the club on weekends, hoping she'd return.

His cell rang, and he glanced down. His lips turned up in a grin despite the hell he knew was sure to come. "Hi, Lucy. How are you?" he asked his sister.

"You haven't called me back!" she chided him. Lucy lived in LA part time, and though she used to stay at Gabe's when she visited New York, with him married, she'd taken to staying at Decklan's. But she hadn't been there in a while.

Last time, she and Max had gotten into some sort of argument, and neither was willing to discuss the reasons behind it. He shrugged. Not his business.

"Hey, Lucy. Sorry, I've been busy."

"Arresting people? Because I'm not sure Gabe's forgiven you for cuffing Isabelle." She snickered into the phone.

He rolled his eyes. Yes, he'd arrested Isabelle before she was Gabe's woman, but in Decklan's defense, there'd been a warrant initiated by her asshole ex accusing her of stealing his car. Not that Decklan had known the details at the time.

"Quit causing trouble, Luce. That's been over for a while."

And he'd bribed himself back into Isabelle's good graces with a bottle of Tums and aggravated his brother at the same time. A win-win, as far as he was concerned.

"Are you okay? Because Gabe says he hasn't heard from you either."

He pinched the bridge of his nose. The one drawback to being close with his siblings was the way Lucy tended to push into his life under the guise of concern. Of course, both he and Gabe would do the same to her if they thought anything was amiss. Nobody would hurt Lucy if they could help it.

"I'm fine." Just avoiding most of humanity and trying to decide what to do about the woman who'd breached his walls. He couldn't get her out of his head.

Lucy huffed, and Decklan could envision the scowl on her face.

"Well, if you don't get back to your usual grouchy self—as opposed to your silent and seriously grouchy self—soon, I'm coming out there to see for myself."

"I hear you. And there's nothing to worry about."

He listened to her catch him up on her life, and finally they said good-bye, him promising to *get his head out of his ass soon.* God, he loved the little brat, he thought with a grin.

He put his phone back in his pocket just as Max arrived, settling into his usual seat. "I have to say, for a man who insists he's not going to renew his membership, you're here all the time lately."

Max knew exactly why Decklan was here, so there was no point in answering.

"If she does show, at least tell me you've got a plan?" Max said, pushing as usual.

"I have no fucking clue."

"Well, I hope you get one." Max slapped him on the back. "I see Emmy giving me the eye. I'm going to go remind her who's the dom," he said. "You ought to find a sub and do the same."

"Have fun," Decklan said, ignoring the suggestion. He wasn't in the mood. Hadn't been for a long time, but especially since *that* night. Since Amanda.

He glanced around the room, familiar with all the spaces and places in the club. The St. Andrews cross on the wall was occupied, a dark-haired female getting pleasure from absorbing pain. His gaze slid onward. A group of men sitting and talking, their subs at their feet. A quick look confirmed she wasn't one of them. His emotions were already frayed tonight, and if he found her with someone else, he couldn't promise himself he'd keep a handle on his temper.

He ordered a Glenlivet on the rocks and tried to put his night with her in perspective. Chemistry. They'd had that in spades. But there was something more to her. A strength combined with a vulnerability he didn't see often. They'd clicked in bed and out. He'd had fun with her, a word he never associated with sex. And most important, the thing that unnerved him the most, she tempted him to want her *touch*. To free her from the restraints so he could feel her soft hands on his cock, her nails at his back, and her arms wrapped securely around him.

Shit. He shouldn't be here. Didn't need that kind of intensity and seriousness in his life.

She wasn't here again, something he took as a sign. Definitely time to go.

He stood, pushed back his chair, turned, and saw Amanda paused at the threshold to the main room. His breath left on a whoosh of air, the unexpected sight of her, when he'd all but given up, a shock to his system.

Over the last few weeks, he wondered if he'd exaggerated the memory of her effect on him. No such luck.

Her head bowed, hands clasped together, she was clearly working up the nerve to enter. And every muscle in his body tightened at the sight.

She finally lifted her gaze and glanced around the room, her stare lingering on various places and people, just as he'd done earlier. And then she looked toward the bar. The sounds

around him, the people, the lights, everything dimmed. There
was only her.

Whatever *it* was, *it* was still there.

He'd waited for this moment, and now that it was here?
Decklan had never backed away from a challenge. He wasn't
about to do so now.

Chapter Six

reathe, breathe, breathe, Amanda told herself. But the very sight of Decklan was both a relief and sent her into panic mode at the same time. His dark eyes slid over her, and for a brief second, she feared he was going to dismiss her. She'd unravel if he did.

Then he slowly walked across the room. All the air left her lungs. She hadn't imagined one thing about him or the intense physical attraction he inspired. Today he wore the same type of outfit, black denim and a black T-shirt that hugged his masculine, well-defined body. She had no doubt he worked out, and she still wanted to feel those hard muscles beneath her hands. If he'd let her.

He strode up, so close she was enveloped in his delicious scent, and all her strategic female parts went on red alert. Her nipples suddenly ached for his hands, his mouth, his teeth.

"Tell me you came here for me," he said, not beating around the bush. At all.

She could deny it and prolong the inevitable, but why bother? "I came here for you," she admitted.

"Any reason to stay?" he asked.

She shook her head.

A low growl of satisfaction escaped his throat, and he grasped her elbow. "Let's go."

When he began his dominant male routine, she fell in line. It was part of what attracted her to him, beyond his stunning looks. He wasn't afraid to be himself, to tell her what he wanted from her, and damned if her body didn't respond. In fact, her sex was throbbing right now.

Add to that that she knew there was a heart inside of him, a man who'd lost his parents at a crucial age, who, like her, held himself apart, and their bond was formed.

The club was located on the east side of Manhattan, discreetly set inside a townhouse where nobody would think twice about what was going on there. Since she hadn't gone into the locker rooms, she hadn't changed into her attire. Leaving was as simple as stepping out the front door.

As soon as they walked outside, the summer heat wafted up from the sidewalk, blanketing her in stifling temperatures.

"Where are we going?" she asked.

"Just walking. For now."

She nodded and noticed he shortened his longer stride to match hers. They weren't far from Fifth Avenue, and he turned there, heading toward Central Park South, which was nearby.

It was heavy and humid, typical Manhattan in the summertime, which explained why so many locals departed for the beaches. She didn't mind the steamy weather, happy to be with the man she'd been having erotic dreams about for weeks. She was also aroused and had been from the minute she'd looked into his hot gaze. His hand, which now rested on her back, merely increased the burn. The silence between them was as thick as the air and just as electrically charged.

She searched for conversation, for a way to get him to open up a little more, but came up empty. If she pushed him for information about himself, he'd likely do the same to her. She sighed, swallowing back frustration that her life wasn't her own. But she'd chosen things this way, and if it meant taking care of Brad the way he did for her, she was okay with that. But she still intended to make the most of whatever time she could grab with Decklan. She deserved at least that.

So much remained unsaid. So much would have to stay locked up inside her.

She stared ahead and caught sight of a horse-drawn carriage. She remembered seeing ads for Christmas in New York City on television as a little girl, and she'd always imagined what it would be like to ride in one. She broke free from Decklan's hold and ran toward the horse, a beautiful animal, shields over its eyes, its operator standing by its side. Behind it, a large covered carriage was attached, waiting for riders.

Decklan caught up with her, pulling her back as she got close to the large animal.

"I've always wanted to take a ride in one of these," she said, feeling every inch the tourist. She didn't care. She clasped her hands together and glanced up at Decklan. "Let's take a ride? Please?"

Decklan took in the woman staring up at him, eyes wide and excited, and found himself unable to deny her wish. Which said something, considering he normally wasn't the kind of man to indulge in frivolous whims or things like horse-drawn carriage rides.

"Okay."

She clapped her hands together like a little kid, so unlike the seductress he'd originally met, and he liked that he was seeing another side of her. While she vibrated with excitement beside him, he discussed the trip with the driver, paying him for extra time, and soon he and Amanda were together in the far back seat of the carriage. The smile on her face as the driver put them in motion made the whole trip worthwhile.

"And we're off." She grinned and shifted next to him. As if he wasn't well aware of her beside him already. His cock had been at full-staff since she'd shown up at the club.

She leaned forward, taking in Central Park at night. "Look at the building lights in the distance. It's so beautiful."

He'd never thought of the city as beautiful before, but with her by his side, he was seeing it that way for the first time.

"Don't they have these in DC?" he asked, still amused by her reaction to something New Yorkers took for granted. And since he'd grown up here, gone to college here, and worked just outside Manhattan, he considered himself a local. He didn't understand Lucy's fascination with LA. He liked the busyness of Manhattan.

"They do," she said. "But my parents never let me go on them."

"Why not?"

She shrugged and shifted in the seat. "It's complicated, but basically my mother wouldn't consider it ladylike. The horses and the carriage would be too filthy for her." She wrinkled her nose, indicating what she thought of her mother's point of view. "She worships perfection."

"Then she must love having you for a daughter," he said, the compliment the most genuine he'd ever given.

Her harsh laugh contradicted him. "That would be a no. I was . . . am . . . everything she doesn't want in a child—especially a girl."

"What the hell?" What she said couldn't have startled him more.

She let out a long sigh, and he wondered if she'd talk or clam up. On the one hand, he wanted to know everything about her, which made him almost hope she'd deflect. Insight into what made her tick was dangerous. He was relaxed, mellow, his walls down, and he was enjoying the evening. It had become way too much like a date without the degree of control he needed to keep his distance.

Yet instead of pulling away, he slid his hand beneath her thick hair and cupped her neck. She moaned and leaned into him. His cock hardened at the sound coming from deep in her throat.

She responded to his subtle command, and without warning, she spoke. "She thinks I'm too big, too curvy, not delicate or ladylike enough. She says I should eat less and exercise more."

"Bullshit."

She flinched at his harsh expletive.

Too damned bad. He'd like to snap her mother's probably scrawny neck for putting such ridiculous thoughts in her daughter's head. And her body-image issues and the need for dim lighting made sense from that warped perspective. And it was warped.

Her curves were the first thing Decklan had noticed. Gorgeous face second. Brain third and sweet personality, which he was just coming to know, fourth, but it was quickly becoming his favorite part of her.

Damn. None of this was good. But he couldn't allow her to let those words remain in her psyche.

"I call bullshit," he told her more clearly, intending to explain just what he thought when he looked at her.

"That's nice of you, but I'm not finished. She also believes that I should marry a man of her choosing and stay home and raise his babies, not work."

Jesus. "That's a helluva lot of expectation heaped on one person."

"I'm used to it."

"I doubt that."

"Well, it doesn't matter. Because we don't speak often." She blew out a long breath and shook her head. "And I have no idea why I dumped all that on you now. That's not what we're about."

"It's not, huh?"

Her lips turned upward. "No, we're about sex. And fun. And right now, this ride is fun."

He didn't argue.

Silence fell around them, the night sky cloaking them in darkness, and the familiar sound of the horse's hooves clicked against the pavement. Time passed in easy silence. Yes, he was aware of her in a base sexual sense, but something else hit him too. A feeling of rightness, making him uncomfortable. He preferred raw desire to this softness, this warmth. He didn't know what to do with the unexpected emotions she brought out in him without even trying.

"I'd love to ride a horse one day," she mused out loud.

A different, more wicked idea took hold. "How about you ride me instead?"

Her eyes opened wide, need reflected in the chocolate orbs. She ran her tongue over her lips, and a jolt of desire licked at him, heightening his need.

"I want that too, but not here."

He agreed. Exhibitionism had its place. This wasn't one of them. He'd only meant it as a tease. And it had worked. Her voice dropped, a slight tremor shook her frame, and her nipples puckered through the silk top.

"But I have to admit, sex in a horse-drawn carriage would be scandalous." She grinned, her smile infectious. "There are other things we can do though." She slid her hand over the bulge in his pants, and his cock, already thick and ready, sprung to further life.

He hissed out a long breath. "Fuck."

"We already decided that wasn't possible in this carriage, but other things are. The way I see it, the driver's up there . . . and there's a blanket right here." She pulled it over his lap. Her eyes held a wealth of passion in their depths, and when she licked her lips, he knew what she intended.

He covered her small hand with his and stilled all motion. "No more."

She blinked at his dominant tone.

Good. Because it was time for him to take charge.

Chapter Seven

*A*manda had operated on autopilot tonight, letting her desire take her where she needed to go. And she wasn't just talking sexual desire. She'd boarded the plane to New York—better judgment be damned—landed, and headed straight for the club. One look at Decklan and she knew why she'd come. To experience the way she felt when he was near. The stomach-churning excitement, the heightened sense of awareness he inspired. All her senses were engaged.

Sight. She couldn't stop staring at him, his tanned, handsome face, white teeth when he deigned to smile, strong jaw, and the integrity she felt he possessed deep inside. *Hearing.* His deep voice caused ripples of awareness throughout her body, drawing her into his orbit, making her wet with his husky commands. *Smell.* Every inhale made her more aware of him as a potent male, and his musky scent that was pure Decklan turned her insides to mush. *Taste.* The memory of his kiss kept her tossing and turning in her bed at night, her nipples hard and begging for his touch and her pussy so wet, she'd have to make herself come with her own hands before she could find any respite in sleep.

And *touch.* Oh God, when he touched her, cupped her neck in his strong hand, she melted, willing to be at his beck and call, even if it meant divulging personal secrets. She shivered at how much she'd revealed to him about her insecurities, but he wasn't using them against her. No, he seemed to embrace the things about her she'd been taught to hate.

The way he waited patiently for her to respond to his command, knowing with certainty she would, allowed her to give over. Although she wanted to touch him further, to outline that hard, thick cock with her hands, gauge his length, and ultimately *taste* him, she stopped all motion and lifted her hand.

"Good girl," he said in a panty-melting voice. "Now hand me your underwear."

She blinked, certain she hadn't heard him correctly.

"Give me your panties." He held out his hand.

She swallowed hard, her sex swelling at the command. "I'm not wearing any."

He let out a shuddering groan. At least she wasn't alone in this whirlpool of need.

"Spread your legs."

She did as he commanded, sliding her thighs apart. At least she'd worn a flirty skirt that hit above the knee, protecting her rear end from the carriage seat.

"More," he ordered.

She spread her legs even wider.

He placed the blanket over the top of her skirt, covering her from prying eyes that didn't exist. At least if the driver turned around, he wouldn't see Decklan's hand beneath the blanket, under her skirt, his fingers skating along her damp outer folds. The roughened pads of his fingertips glided along her sensitized flesh.

"Oh God," she moaned aloud.

"Shh. I don't want to have to gag you."

Gag her? Here?

"You'll be quiet?" he asked in that dark voice that gave her a rush.

She nodded quickly.

He kissed her jaw, licked her pulse point, and continued to tease her slick sex. "You're beautiful."

She shook her head—out of habit—and he pinched her clit. Pain radiated through her core.

"Are you calling me a liar?" he asked.

She shook her head. Tears threatened. Not because he'd hurt her physically. No, that pain had almost immediately grown into something hot and sweet. Something good. She wasn't really sure why the emotional tears were ready to come.

"Then believe what I'm saying. You're gorgeous. Do you want to know the first thing I noticed about you? Your curves," he continued without waiting for her to reply.

He shifted in his seat. One hand covered her mound, and as he ground his palm against her sex, waves of wonderful sensation took her to another, higher plane. She floated on the cloud of passion he created, his large hand causing ripples of desire to coil tighter and tighter around her.

And with his other hand? He reached beneath her shirt and cupped one breast hard. "They were so lush and full," he said, tweaking her nipple with his fingers, pulling at the already aching, distended peak. Moisture flooded from her sex into his waiting hand.

He groaned his approval. Slid one finger inside her wet heat. Her inner walls clamped around him, and she bit back a moan. All the while, he continued to talk, his sexy voice lulling her into that quiet space in her head where all that mattered was him, that he liked what he saw in her, and that she believed him.

"They were so big and full," he said, bringing her back to herself. Talking about her body tended to do that. "And ripe, plumping over the corset, just made for me to stroke, lick . . . and bite."

He pinched her nipple, and the pain had a direct line to her pussy, the need so deep that she threw her head back and gritted her teeth to suppress a scream.

"I wondered if your nipples were rose-colored or peach." He added a second finger, thrusting into her along with the first. "But then I got distracted by your ass. Those cheeks are made for my hands. I wanted to squeeze those globes so hard, I'd see handprints the next day and know you're mine. Know that I thrust deep inside your wet pussy and felt you grind and clench around me while you came."

As he spoke, he pressed hard against her clit, and she bucked into his hand, rotating her hips, seeking deeper, more constant contact. He didn't stop her. Didn't seem to mind her frenzied state. Merely met her desire with a third finger, harder thrusts. "Like I said, so damned beautiful."

She whimpered and rocked against his hand, his fingers filling her, her harsh pants loud to her ears. He ground his hand in small circles, and she built toward climax, the fresh air around her, the *clickety-clack* of the horse's hooves, the city sounds all blurring together in her head.

"Oh God."

"Yes," he said through clenched teeth. "That's it. Ride me," he whispered darkly in her ear. "Just like that horse you want to ride. Take what you need."

She rocked her pelvis around and around against his hard hand, the pressure building. So close. "I'm coming!"

Just as she was about to scream, he clamped a hand over her mouth, the unexpected action necessary to preserve their privacy, but it was hot and erotic at the same time. Her entire body lost to sensation and the pressure of his hand hard against her mound, her hips gyrating in never-ending circles. She came, the most exquisite climax of her life overtaking her.

The cab that returned them to the club after the carriage ride was an exercise in pure frustration for Decklan, while a satisfied Amanda curled into his side. The drive from Manhattan to his house was even more difficult. Amanda dozed in the passenger seat, leaving him surrounded by her delicious scent and with an erection that needed to be handled. Soon.

If the physical ache were his only issue, he'd be set. But Amanda had done the impossible. She'd made her way inside him, and he'd already accepted this was a hell of a lot more than a one-night stand. Was this how Gabe had felt on meeting Isabelle? If so, Decklan was finally beginning to understand how his solitary brother had become obsessed, engaged, and ultimately married.

Amanda was chipping away at boundaries Decklan had always thought he needed to live, breathe, and just *be*. He needed control. She shredded his. He'd refused to care about anyone but his siblings. He didn't allow women close, but she'd gotten in. He cared.

He wanted to ease the pain of the young girl whose mother had done severe damage to her self-esteem and be there for the beautiful woman she'd become. Not that she knew or accepted the truth about herself, and maybe that was part of her appeal. He recognized her vulnerability because it ran deep inside him too. She feared she couldn't be loved as is. He feared love because it meant he could be left and shattered again. With every minute that passed, he was afraid it was too late to halt the inevitable.

Once he parked, he woke Amanda and kept her close as he guided her up to his apartment. An older couple joined them in the elevator, and he clenched his jaw during the slow ride up, placing Amanda in front of him, blocking any view of his obvious erection. It hurt like hell, his cock pressed hard and ready against the confining denim.

The moment his apartment door closed behind him, Decklan's control snapped. He lifted Amanda and settled her on the heavy oak dining room table.

"Something tells me this isn't the intended use of furniture," she said, a sexy grin lifting her lips.

He shrugged. "I don't know about that. It's for eating, isn't it?" He lifted her skirt and slid her toward him, parting and holding her thighs open with both hands.

Her glistening pussy lips beckoned, and he leaned down, treating himself to a thorough lick of her delicious juices.

A shudder shook her frame. "Oh, Decklan."

The sound of his name was hell on his restraint, but he managed to hang on. She arched her hips toward his mouth, and he nibbled at her, teasing, tasting, biting, bringing her to the brink before deliberately stopping.

"Please, no. Don't stop," she practically wailed, her body trembling beneath him as she fought against his firm grip on her legs.

He nuzzled her thighs with his nose and mouth, then released her long enough to pull a condom from his pocket. He unzipped his jeans and shed them in one smooth shove down his legs. He covered himself quickly and grasped her legs once more. A low, shuddering sound escaped her throat, impaling him with a deep sense of satisfaction.

Because he liked holding on to her, he realized. Though he enjoyed the power he possessed, it wasn't the same sense of control he normally sought. This was a different kind of satisfaction. One that came from knowing she craved his touch, craved *him* as much as he did her.

It was mutual. And that mattered to him for the first time. The urge to thrust into her was strong, but so was the unusual urge to tease, play, and please her again. He grasped his cock in one hand and ran the length along her wet, needy sex.

She sucked in a shallow breath. Her body bucked on the table. He didn't let up, teasing her clit, gliding his hard erection over and over the tiny bud that gave so much pleasure.

"You like that?" he asked.

She moaned a reply.

He chuckled through gritted teeth and circled his cock over her damp mound, pushing himself down harder, deliberately stimulating her to the point of no return. She slapped her hands against the tabletop, her back arched, her body convulsing as low groans accompanied her climax.

He had her just where he wanted her, lost to sensation, but waited until the tremors ebbed before parting her sex with his fingertips and pressing the head of his cock home. She was slick and ready for him yet still tight. He slid out and pressed in once more, feeling the drag and pull as he plunged in, his body snug and buried inside her.

He glanced down, taking in the sight of her gripping and holding him. "Look."

She pushed onto her elbows. Glanced down, her chocolate eyes full of need.

"So fucking good, right? Watch us." He slid out slowly, his cock damp with her arousal, then thrust back. In. Out. In. Out.

"God, Decklan. I feel all of you." She bent her knees, bracing her feet against the table, sighing in pleasure as the move sucked him in deeper.

Shit, she undid him. His emotions raw, his body on fire—the time for play was over.

"Hang on, baby." He gripped her hips and hammered into her, her body sliding on the table, only his hands keeping her in place.

If he thought for a second he was hurting her, he'd let up, but her cries were of passion, and damn, they were hot. She clenched around him, milking his cock with her hot pussy. He wasn't going to last long and wanted her with him when he blew.

He was so damned close; sweat slickened his skin, and he drove into her once, twice, and on the third time, he slid a hand between them and pressed on her clit. That's all it took. She convulsed around him, and he stilled against her, spilling everything he had inside her.

As he shook with aftershocks, still catching his breath, she clasped her hands around his wrists. He caught his breath, his immediate instinct to pull free.

"Oh God, I'm still coming." She ground herself against him, her small hands gripping him, her nails digging into his skin.

And suddenly what a woman wanted during sex meant more than what he'd always thought he needed.

Chapter Eight

*A*manda woke up naked, sore but exquisitely happy. A hot, sexy man who'd more than satisfied her sexually lay sleeping by her side. There was something so strong about Decklan. Beyond the physical, she felt like they connected on a more intimate level. So much so that she'd revealed things about her childhood and her mother that she'd never told anyone else in her life. Except Brad, and that had been a long time ago.

She almost wished . . . Nope, she wouldn't go there. She had the weekend to herself, and she intended to make the most of it by enjoying and not dwelling on things she couldn't have. At least not without hurting people she cared about in the process.

Decklan rolled over to his back on a big groan. A glance told her he was still out cold. His profile was as strong in sleep as awake, but there was something more vulnerable about him. That vulnerability called to her, tugged at her emotions and, again, made her want to dig deeper . . . which wasn't fair.

So she cut that thought off and focused on a more fun one. He'd kicked off his side of the covers and lay sprawled naked for her hungry gaze. His skin was tanned to a golden glow, a slight dusting of dark hair covered his chest, and his muscles were impressive. Her gaze traveled downward. Another light sprinkling of hair took a path south, leading to his impressive hardening erection. It was as if he was aware of her gaze, even in sleep.

She was tempted to lie down on top of him and bring him awake slowly, then inch downward and take him into her mouth. She moaned at the thought. But she respected his need for lack of touch, and so she changed her mind and aligned her body against his side instead.

She briefly rested her cheek against his forearm, closing her eyes and soaking in how right she felt here, with him. A small kiss on his roughened skin and then she tucked her head into his shoulder.

He shifted, but before she could ask if he was awake, the doorbell rang, jarring them both.

She rolled over and looked at him. "Morning."

His eyes darkened as they locked on her.

Then the doorbell did its thing again.

"God, who'd show up here so early? I'm off this weekend, and I really don't want any interruptions."

Another ring told them the person wasn't going away.

"I'm up," he said without moving.

His erection twitched against his stomach.

"Yes, you are," she said, laughing.

He rose, grumbling, and pulled on a pair of sweats hanging over a chair in the corner. She followed the long line of his muscular back and sighed.

"Stay here. I'll get rid of them and be right back."

Decklan strode down the hall, pissed at the interruption. He didn't have many full weekends off, and he definitely didn't spend the ones he did with the only woman he wanted in his bed.

He reached his front door and swung it open. "Go away," he said, not caring who was there.

"What a way to greet family," his brother Gabe said, grinning, his arm around his wife.

"Hi. And bye?" Isabelle waved a hand, blushing.

"Nope. We're here, we're staying." Gabe pushed past him, pulling Isabelle along with him. "We have news."

"And you couldn't have called?" Decklan asked, folding his arms across his bare chest.

"It wouldn't have been as much fun. What's got you in such a mood?"

"We woke him," his pretty wife said.

"She's smart. Not that smart since she's with you, but she did catch on quickly."

"I'm thinking you have company." Gabe smirked, enjoying being the pain in the ass that he was.

Isabelle tugged on Gabe's arm. "We should go. We'll call you later and fill you in."

Decklan sighed and stepped back into the apartment. "No, come on in. You drove all the way out here. What's up?" he asked grudgingly.

"You're going to be an uncle," Gabe said, placing his hand over Isabelle's flat stomach. "Forgive me for thinking you'd want to hear the news in person."

His brother's happiness was both a blessing and a punch in the gut to Decklan, who'd never let himself think of having a wife or kids of his own. Lucy and Gabe were his family. He'd welcomed Isabelle because she made his brother happy, but it left him odd man out. He hadn't let himself feel it too much—Decklan preferred not to feel at all—but now, a baby? His brother would be having his own family—one that didn't include him.

"Congratulations," he said with a combination of genuine and forced cheer.

He really sucked, he thought. Knowing how thrilled his brother was, he ought to feel exactly the same way. He pulled Isabelle into a brotherly hug, not wanting to give Gabe the chance to catch on that anything was wrong. Given time to adjust to the news, he'd be just fine.

"Thanks." She squeezed him back. "Are you okay?" she whispered in his ear.

"I'm good. Promise."

Gabe grabbed Decklan's shoulder and physically separated the two. "Enough hugging."

Decklan rolled his eyes, and Isabelle laughed. "Back off, caveman. He's my brother too."

He grinned, pleased he could at least annoy Gabe as much as his brother could bug him.

"Hi," Amanda said, joining them.

Decklan glanced her way. She wore a pretty yellow sundress she must have had rolled in her bag, her feet were bare, and she hadn't added makeup. Her hair fell around her shoulders. No artifice, no pretense. She'd never looked more beautiful.

"Am I interrupting?" she asked.

"Of course not."

Except she was. He never introduced his brother to the women he was involved with. Because he never got involved. But he was now. And looking at her merely confirmed it. Not just because she affected him sexually, which she did, but because the vulnerability in her gaze tugged at his heart. And he really hadn't thought he had one to speak of.

Gabe studied her through hooded eyes, clearly doing his assessment thing. Isabelle, though—she looked from Decklan to the other woman, and a big grin showed on her face.

There was nothing to do but introduce them. "Amanda Collins, this is my brother, Gabe, and his wife, Isabelle."

"Hi," Amanda said, more shyly than he would have expected.

"Hi!" Isabelle walked up to her and gave a warm smile that welcomed her right away. "I'm happy to meet you."

"Umm . . . same. And thanks." Amanda ran a hand through her hair, clearly uncomfortable.

"We didn't mean to interrupt, but Gabe and I came to tell Decklan he's going to be an uncle." She excitedly tapped at her belly.

Her cheeks were glowing, happiness just exuded from her in contagious waves, and Decklan couldn't help but feel and share her joy.

"That's great!" Amanda said in a shaky voice. "Congratulations. Listen, I can see this is a family moment. I'll call a cab and be out of here in a few minutes. Then you can all celebrate." She turned away and started for the bedroom.

"No!" All three of them spoke loudly and at the same time. Even Decklan was startled.

Amanda paused and glanced over her shoulder.

"Don't leave on our account," Gabe said. "I would love to get to know my brother's—" His words ended with a sharp jab to his stomach by his pregnant wife.

And Decklan blew out a relieved breath, grateful Isabelle had stepped in. He didn't know what he and Amanda were yet. And fuck Gabe for trying to push him into admitting something. Just because his brother was ready for a wife, a baby, and the whole white picket fence thing didn't mean Decklan was.

Except he couldn't stop thinking about that tiny thing growing inside his sister-in-law. He was going to be an uncle, Gabe a father. And the more he let it sink in, the more excited he became.

"Stay," he heard himself saying to Amanda. Because this was an important moment in his life, and he wanted her to share it with him.

His mouth suddenly ran dry at the thought. If asked, he'd have said he wasn't ready to have Amanda mingling with his family, but now that it was happening? He was happy. And relieved it was done. Because as short as their time had been together, she was coming to mean something to him.

So he didn't want her leaving now, embarrassed because she'd spent the night. And he sure as hell wasn't prepared to give up his time with her. Obviously Gabe and Iz weren't leaving any time soon, so the solution was clear.

She met his gaze, as if searching his expression to make sure she was welcome.

"Stay," he said again, more firmly this time, so she understood he knew this was his choice.

She exhaled long and hard. "Okay, then."

"Great! Now that that's settled, breakfast, anyone?" Isabelle asked, her cheery voice interrupting any silent moment he and Amanda might have been sharing.

"Isabelle, I'm not sure they want company," Gabe said.

She waved a hand at him. "Nonsense, right, Decklan?" she asked before anyone could reply. "We can go to that cute place down the road. They have the best pancakes. And French toast. Blintzes. And bacon."

Gabe snorted a laugh.

"What?" she asked, offended. "I'm eating for two."

"Kitten, watching you eat is my favorite pastime." Gabe smiled at her indulgently, the whole scene so at odds with the man he'd been. Isabelle had changed Gabe for the better.

"No morning sickness?" Amanda asked.

Isabelle shook her head. "Not really. Just a little at odd times." She glanced at Decklan. "We figured it out on Eden when we were there for the opening of Elite. But I wanted to keep it quiet until we were sure."

"Now she can't wait to share it with the world," Gabe said, wrapping an arm protectively around her.

Decklan watched his brother and sister-in-law through new eyes. Now that he had someone in his life who interested him beyond one night, he wasn't so quick to call his brother whipped. He was more intrigued by their dynamic. Panicked at the thought of feeling as much as Gabe did, but he didn't have to rush things. He just had to see where things with Amanda led.

"I'm happy for you both," Amanda said, but the way she rubbed her arms, her discomfort was clear.

"If we're going out, we need to get ready," Decklan said, having decided to get her alone and make sure she was comfortable with breakfast and the idea of company.

Once in the bedroom, Amanda realized her heart was pounding hard in her chest. She'd never thought the doorbell was family. A neighbor maybe, and when Decklan had taken his time coming back to her, she'd decided to see what was holding him up.

His brother and pregnant wife. Now breakfast. How had things gotten so complicated so fast? This was an affair—meant to be fun, not serious, and meeting family first thing the morning after was *serious*.

She turned toward him, ignoring the direct hit, both physical and emotional, that she took upon looking at him. "You should go with your brother and his wife. They have a lot to celebrate." She gathered her purse. "Like I said, I can take a cab back to the city."

He stared at her, and she couldn't read him. Uncomfortable, she pulled her cell from her purse and began to Google taxicabs in the area.

"Don't." Decklan's voice startled her. "You should come with us."

She blinked. "What? *Why?*"

"You need to eat, for one thing. And for another, maybe if you're there, they won't grill me mercilessly." He winked at her.

"Oh, I should come to be your buffer?" she asked, glad he'd turned things light.

He shrugged. "You're also good to look at." His eyes darkened as his gaze raked her over.

She felt herself flush but was beyond pleased with the compliment. "Then we should get ready," she said, blurting the words out before she could think them through or change her mind.

Though she hadn't planned on breakfast with the family, one meal couldn't hurt, no matter how domestic. She swallowed hard because she was lying to herself. It could hurt. She already felt too much for this man. As for his brother, she couldn't read Gabe at all, but she liked Isabelle's warmth and friendly charm.

One breakfast. That was all. Then she wouldn't see them again. With a determined nod, she took a quick shower, washed her hair and pulled it into a wet, messy bun, dressed, and washed her face. She had the extracrinkly cotton dress she'd rolled into her bag and nothing more. No makeup to help her look more presentable, but she didn't have a choice.

"Ready?" Decklan asked, his gaze eating her up and making her feel more beautiful than she ever could be.

Her gaze slid over him. In a pair of faded jeans and a pale-blue T-shirt, his hair damp, face unshaven, he looked deliciously sexy. And because he'd showered too, he smelled deliciously sexy. Yum.

She nodded. "Ready." As she would ever be.

He took her hand and led her from the room.

To her surprise, she enjoyed the next few hours. Decklan's family was fun—well, Isabelle was. Gabe liked to brood and stare, as if he could get into Amanda's head and see what she was hiding. But his wife? In the short time they were all together, Isabelle had managed to exchange phone numbers with Amanda, press her for plans the next time she was in New York, and show her another side of Decklan.

Isabelle and Decklan had an amusing relationship. "He didn't really arrest you, did he?" Amanda asked as the men were arguing over paying the check.

"He certainly did." Isabelle stared at her with wide blue eyes. "I'd just left my ex's place for good. I found a video of him cheating on me," she said, her voice lowered. "But it really had been over for a while. Anyway, I drove off in the rain in my Mercedes, and Lance, the bastard, reported the car stolen."

Amanda stared, dumbfounded. "Who does something like that?" she asked.

"A pompous son of a bitch," Gabe muttered, now in tune with the conversation.

Isabelle merely nodded at his assessment. "I didn't put things together right away, but turns out that my arresting officer"—she pointed to Decklan—"was Gabe's brother. I knew Gabe from the country club my ex belonged to. Anyway, Gabe showed up to see Decklan, and there I was cuffed to the desk—"

"Because my brother doesn't know the best places to bind a woman," Gabe said with a smirk, the first real joke the other man had made.

"He does so!" Amanda said, defending Decklan.

Until she realized exactly what she'd admitted to and shared with the man's family. Strangers to her. Her cheeks flamed with embarrassed heat.

Gabe grinned, showing her the family smile and resemblance for the first time. "Glad to know you have it in you, little brother."

Isabelle punched him lightly in the arm and shot Amanda a sympathetic smile. "They can be major pains in the ass." She leaned in closer. "But it's worth it in bed, isn't it?"

Oh dear Lord. Amanda managed a nod, but her head was spinning with the implications of what they'd all just shared. Wasn't that what friends did? Family? How had she become a part of all this so quickly?

"I think we should get back to Isabelle's arrest," Decklan said, his understanding gaze on Amanda's face. He obviously picked up on her discomfort, and he didn't look too thrilled with his brother himself. She appreciated how he'd turned the conversation away from the too-personal sharing of information.

"It all worked out okay," Isabelle said. "Decklan brought me an apology gift."

Amanda raised an eyebrow. "He did?"

"Tums," the other woman said with a grin.

"Suck-up," Gabe muttered with a roll of his eyes.

Obviously it was an inside joke, but it served to show her how close this family was, and unexpected warmth curled in her belly. So opposite of the dysfunction she'd grown up with. In her family, the differences of opinion weren't fun or treated like jokes. Instead, barbs were thrown by her mother at every turn.

At that thought, her phone rang. "Excuse me," she said, pulling her cell from her purse and glancing down. "God, it's like she has ESP or something." Amanda hit ignore on her mother's call.

"Everything okay?" Decklan asked.

She nodded. "Just my mother. It can wait."

He narrowed his gaze but said nothing.

"So, Isabelle, will you find out the sex of the baby?" Amanda asked, desperate to keep the focus off of herself.

Isabelle immediately reached for Gabe's hand. "I think I want to know. That way I can plan the nursery and layette." Her voice pitched in excitement.

And for the first time ever, a feeling of extreme longing overtook Amanda.

Chapter Nine

*A*manda and Decklan didn't talk about his family, but he seemed content after the breakfast. His brother and wife left, and they spent the rest of the rainy day watching movies on Netflix and just hanging out like a normal couple. Which scared her, because she enjoyed their time together so much, going home would be difficult this time.

He didn't bring up the subject of her leaving, and neither did she. Instead, they ordered in dinner and enjoyed one another in bed. He cuffed her to the headboard, his dark-blue gaze hot on hers, as he brought her to orgasm after orgasm before filling her body with his. Prior to Decklan, she'd been satisfied with meaningless encounters, but they connected on a deep, intimate level. One that'd grown stronger after she'd met and spent time with his family.

As the sunlight streamed through his bedroom window, Amanda studied his handsome face, memorizing each feature. She wished she had better answers to what she wanted. Needed. Instead, she had him for a little while longer.

She leaned close, about to brush a kiss over his lips and wake him up, when, without warning, he came awake with a yell, jerking into an upright position.

"Are you okay?" she asked, reaching for him. He withdrew, lying back down but not touching her.

"Yeah. I was dreaming." He grew silent, obviously remembering.

"Can you talk about it?" Would he?

Decklan stared into the face of the woman who'd made him feel again. She waited patiently, her beautiful face watching him, staring at him thoughtfully. Expectantly.

He didn't owe her anything, least of all an explanation, yet he found himself starting to speak. "I was dreaming about the night my parents died." He hadn't had this dream in years. It had begun when he was nineteen and had suddenly found himself dealing with shocking and profound loss.

"They were killed driving home from Gabe's college graduation. We'd all taken separate cars because I wanted to go out with my friends. Lucy wanted to ride in the front, so she came with me, and Gabe stayed at school to hang with his friends one last time." Decklan swallowed, but his throat was dry.

The memory assaulting him hurt his chest, impacting his breathing. "If I hadn't wanted to go out, we'd have been in the same car. An eighteen-wheeler barreled into them. They didn't have a chance."

"Oh God." Amanda placed a hand on his shoulder.

He didn't flinch, finding unexpected comfort in her touch. "Afterward, I felt so out of control. I'd have these horrible nightmares. That I was in the car and being suffocated by wreckage. I'd wake up thrashing and screaming." Gabe used to shake him back to reality, and he'd be covered in sweat, breathing hard.

He blew out a harsh breath. "That's what happened this morning. That dream." He hung his head, not wanting to think about that suffocating feeling of losing everyone and everything. At least, that's what it had felt like at the time and what he experienced over and over during each awful dream.

"Decklan?" Amanda asked, her sweet voice ripping something open inside him. He didn't know how to handle this kind of emotional discussion or the turmoil beating at him.

"Would you rather be alone?" she asked into the silence surrounding them.

He reached out a hand and grasped her wrist. "No." She'd be leaving this afternoon anyway. His heart sped up inside his chest at the thought of her gone. Though it would be a hell of a lot easier to let her leave, he couldn't. He needed her.

Admitting that ripped apart something inside him. Before he could allow himself to think things through, he had her flat on her back, his naked and now fully aroused body coming down on top of her.

He met her gaze. Her lips parted, eyes glazed. She was with him. He gritted his teeth and thrust deep, her tight walls clenching around him. She raised her hands and grasped the headboard of her own volition. He pounded into her. She lifted her hips, meeting him with each thrust, taking him deeper.

He wasn't going to last. Not when he felt the familiar tingle in the base of his spine, signaling he was close. But he wasn't coming alone. He slid his hand between them and pinched her clit. She threw her head back and called out his name, her body convulsing, her orgasm a hell of a sight to see. Seconds later, he came hard, losing himself inside her warm, willing body, all thoughts of the past gone—for now.

Breathing hard, he rolled to his side and curled her into him. This felt good. Right.

"Decklan, just so you know, I'm on the pill."

Her words slammed into him, shocking him to his core. "Shit. I didn't even think." He'd been too far gone emotionally. "I'm sorry. I swear I'm clean."

"The club requires tests. I know." Which explained why she was so much calmer than him. *She* was thinking clearly.

She touched his cheek. "It's okay."

But he broke into a sweat, knowing how stupidly irresponsible he'd been. For a man who prided himself on control, he'd certainly had none a few minutes ago.

He managed a nod. "Okay."

They lay in silence, his heart beating hard, the nightmare and what he'd stupidly done torturing him.

"Hey." She curled into him, and he pulled her back into his arms. "I'm here."

He knew. And maybe that's why he was able to fall back to sleep. Later, they woke up and, by silent agreement, took separate showers because they were starving and needed to go eat, not get distracted. Neither spoke of his nightmare, for which he was grateful.

While she was in the shower, he'd picked up her phone and programmed his number into it, then added her cell phone number to the contacts in his phone. Decklan was invested in her now, and he didn't want to risk another monthlong lapse once she returned to DC and he had too much time to think.

They'd returned to the same restaurant they'd eaten at with Isabelle and Gabe and ordered breakfast. While waiting for the food, she'd excused herself to use the ladies' room. The waiter arrived with their dishes just as Amanda returned.

As she headed his way, he found himself unable to draw his gaze from the sexy sway of her hips. He had it bad, and he knew it. Maybe it had been Gabe's and Isabelle's easy acceptance of Amanda, or maybe it had been how perfectly she'd meshed with them that had sealed the deal. But this was no longer casual for him. At all.

She picked up the chocolate croissant she'd ordered and took a bite, closing her eyes and groaning as she began to chew. "God, this is delicious."

He grinned. "You're cute." He reached out and wiped a smudge of chocolate off her lower lip.

Her lashes fluttered, and her eyes darkened at his touch. Then her tongue darted out, and she licked his finger with the tip.

Sparks flew directly to his groin. "You're playing with fire, you know. We're in public. And you have more issues with public displays than I do."

She cleared her throat. "I was just acting on impulse." She raised her shoulder in a tiny shrug.

He groaned and shifted in his seat, his jeans now uncomfortably tight. "I like when you're impulsive." He paused, then added, "I like you."

A pink flush stained her cheeks, and she looked away.

Okay, so she wasn't ready. A hard pang hit him in the chest. He'd just have to lead her there. He had no doubt he could do it. Their chemistry and interaction was special.

"So tell me about your life in Washington," he said, changing the subject.

She relaxed, her shoulders easing down as she leaned in, chin propped on her hand. And she proceeded to regale him with stories about living in Washington, DC, and about her friends at home—in particular, her best friend with whom she worked.

Decklan was grateful to finally be let in and listened intently.

"I'm his personal assistant, girl Friday, whatever you want to call it. When he gets lost in computer code, someone has to make sure he lifts his head long enough to eat, take a break, or even leave for the night." She shook her head and smiled fondly. "He's always been like the absentminded professor."

Decklan's gut tightened at the warmth in her voice. "He's just your boss?" He needed to hear her reassure him.

She raised her gaze, obviously startled by his question. "We go way back, actually. We met in college."

"And he's never made a play?" Because a guy would have to be dead not to look at Amanda and want her.

She burst out laughing, then sobered when she obviously realized he wasn't joining in.

She wrinkled her nose at him, her perceptive gaze narrowing. "If I didn't know better, I'd think your jealous streak was showing."

"What makes you think it isn't?" he asked, suddenly feeling extremely possessive where she was concerned.

Her eyes opened wide. "You can't—We can't—"

"We can." He couldn't hold back. Refused to. "This"—he gestured between them—"doesn't happen every day. Believe me, I know." He'd never felt a connection with a woman before in his life, never mind the intensity of the feelings she'd brought out in him in such a short time.

He wasn't about to let her slip through his fingers because she was afraid. If he could fight his fears, she could damn well do the same. And he'd be there to help her.

She picked up her coffee and took a sip, her hands shaking badly.

"It might have happened fast, but can you tell me you don't feel the same way?" he asked, knowing he was pushing, probably too hard, but he didn't care.

She slammed the ceramic cup down, and it wobbled in the saucer. "I can't. It's complicated, and I really need to go." She scrambled for her small purse and rose, heading for the door.

"Dammit." He tossed money on the table and rushed out after her.

He caught up with her at the corner just as she'd pulled out her cell phone and had begun to dial.

He grabbed her arm. "What's going on?"

She spun to face him, eyes wide and panicked. "This was supposed to be easy and fun. No strings. Now I'm meeting family, and you're talking about more than a good time."

"Things changed," he bit out, letting his frustration get the better of him. "Unless I'm mistaken?"

While waiting for her answer, he fought the fear of loss that normally held him captive. One part of him argued that he'd opened his soul to her and she was rejecting him, leaving him alone, and the cold freeze he usually lived in tried to wrap itself around his heart.

Her shoulders slumped, and she shook her head. "No, you're not mistaken," she whispered. "I feel the same way. I just . . . I need to think. I need time."

He released the breath he'd been unaware of holding. He didn't ask how much time. He'd give her some leeway, as difficult as it would be. Especially since their time apart really was apart—as in two different cities. But he intended to find out what had her freaked. And find a way around any problem.

Chapter Ten

*T*he following week, Decklan worked long shifts, hoping to lose himself in other people's arrests and issues instead of his own. Now, on his Thursday off, he met his brother at Gabe's favorite gym. Normally a game of hoops would knock the tension off his shoulders. Not today.

Not since Amanda had left for DC, and silence had followed. Though he'd made sure to get her phone number, he wasn't sure of the response he'd get should he call. And he didn't know what to do in order to change her mind and convince her to give a real relationship a try.

He wiped the sweat from his forehead with a towel and tossed it onto the bench by his locker, then fought with his key card and the combination lock. It took three freaking tries to get into his locker.

His thoughts were consumed by a woman, something he wasn't used to. He missed her. Another foreign feeling. Her scent lingered in his sheets, and he looked forward to bed more than was normal. He just didn't know whether to push hard or give her the space she'd said she needed. He'd even considered a surprise visit, but he didn't have her address. Again, he could find it, no problem, but she might consider the invasion of privacy a deal breaker. He didn't want to give her another reason to run. Not that he knew what really had her scared in the first place.

"You planning on PMSing for the rest of the night?" Gabe flicked him with the end of his towel like he used to do when they were kids.

"Shut up." Decklan wasn't in the mood for Gabe's shit. Which meant maybe he was acting like a girl. *Fuck.*

"Does your mood have something to do with Amanda?" Gabe asked, leaning one foot on the bench between the lockers. "Iz liked her. I'm reserving judgment because I don't know her well enough yet. But considering my wife asked Amanda to go shopping next time she's in town, I'm assuming that will change."

"Isabelle did *what?*" How had she been in touch with Amanda when Decklan hadn't?

Gabe laughed at that. Decklan hadn't even realized he'd said that last part out loud.

"Apparently, the women exchanged phone numbers while we weren't paying attention. And since Isabelle seems to think she's *the one*, she wants to get to know her better." Gabe shrugged. "Regardless, it's not like you to let some chick mess with your head."

Decklan's head was spinning, but he held on to the thread of conversation enough to answer his brother's stupid comment. "Amanda's not just some chick," he snapped back.

Which had been the problem from the minute he'd laid eyes on her.

Gabe chuckled. "Yeah, well, I already figured that out."

"You always were the quick one," Decklan muttered.

Decklan took more time, thought things through before acting. Yet Amanda, who he'd known a short time, already had him rethinking what he believed in and thought he wanted out of life. Everything that had been enough for him suddenly wasn't. He no longer wanted to be a man trapped by the fear of loss. And he desired more than the solitary existence he'd carved out for himself so far.

Hell, he wanted what Gabe and Isabelle had, something Decklan had discovered during the short breakfast he'd spent with his family and with Amanda.

"What's changed?" Gabe asked.

A man of few words, Gabe always left Decklan to sort out the meaning of the question for himself and come up with his own answer to whatever spin or interpretation he chose.

Decklan lowered himself onto the wooden bench, and Gabe joined him. He thought of his chosen life, his lack of dating, the first time he'd gone to a BDSM club and discovered a lifestyle that suited him. Not one he'd shared with his older sibling.

"After Mom and Dad died, I never wanted to give up control—of my emotions." And more.

Gabe nodded. "I get that. I lived life the same way."

As Decklan knew, Gabe had tried marriage once and suffered a tragic loss. Afterward, Gabe had chosen women he couldn't possibly love and kept his relationships cold. Until Isabelle.

"And control works for a while. Until you realize it doesn't keep you warm at night. Neither do women you tie up and never let get close," Gabe added in a knowing voice, forcing Decklan to meet his gaze.

"I never thought we had that in common," Decklan said, still surprised.

"We never talked about it." Gabe shrugged. "You think I didn't know you have the same control issues I do?"

"I didn't realize we dealt with them the same way."

Gabe inclined his head. "Whatever works works. Until it doesn't anymore. Are you still dreaming?" he asked.

Decklan groaned at the reminder of this weekend. "Just started up again."

"Because of her. Because she's gotten in. She makes you emotionally vulnerable, like you were after Mom and Dad died."

Decklan shivered at the reminder. "How do you figure this shit out so easily?"

"I'm older. Wiser. Lived through more before I came out the other end."

He admired his brother—he really did. "And how did you manage that? Coming out the other end, I mean?"

"Once Iz got through my walls, she was in. My problem was keeping her there. I sense you have the same problem?"

Decklan nodded. "How'd you get Isabelle to come around?"

"Different situation. Isabelle needed to know she could trust me to let her live and breathe, to be independent. Then she needed for me to really let her in. That's not your problem. You've got a woman living in another city."

"And she keeps everything wrapped tight inside her." Which meant she was keeping herself emotionally apart from him.

Gabe rose and paced the empty locker room. "Do you think she's hiding something? I can find out anything you want to know. Then you can make the problem go away."

Decklan rolled his eyes. "I'm a cop. I can do the same thing. But no, I don't think she's hiding something big. She's just got issues. Who doesn't?"

"Then go all out. Balls to the wall. See if you can win her over. If that doesn't work, back off and wait for her to come to you." He paused. "And if *that* doesn't work, lure her to Fantasy Island." Gabe grinned and flicked the damned towel again.

Decklan jumped up and out of the way in time. "In other words, try everything?"

Gabe grinned. "You said it, brother."

Decklan didn't know which approach to try first. He'd spooked her the other day by changing the rules. Well, hell.

He'd spooked himself. But now that he knew what he wanted, he had no problem taking risks.

And Amanda just might be the biggest risk of all.

Amanda finished scheduling Brad's speaking engagement at an upcoming conference and updated his calendar both online and by hand. She had a to-do list a mile long, and her mind wasn't on task. How could it be?

Amanda couldn't get Decklan out of her mind. The confused man who'd lost his parents and locked himself behind impenetrable walls. And the heartbreaking man who had trusted her and let her in. He played her body well, but the truth was, in a short time, he'd gotten into her head as well. As for her heart . . .

Her cell phone rang before she could finish that thought, and she grabbed it without checking the screen. "Hello?"

"Morning, sunshine."

Amanda's skin warmed at the low, sexy tone of Decklan's voice. Then her heart skipped a few beats. "How did you get my number?"

"I have my ways. I wasn't letting you disappear for a h this time."

She hesitated, then said, "I'm glad."

"Good to know, considering how we left things."

She swallowed hard. "Yes, I believe I asked for time."

"Time will only let you think too hard. So how have you been keeping busy?" he asked, changing the subject. *Smart man*, she thought.

"Working. Lunch with some girlfriends. The usual."

"Well, that's the thing. I don't know what your usual is. And I'd like to."

She panicked at the thought but only because she couldn't imagine her two lives colliding. But it was only days, and she missed him already. "What are you thinking?"

"That I have time off coming to me, and I'd like to come to visit."

She ran her tongue over her lips. "Umm . . ."

"Nothing heavy," he promised. "We can spend time alone like we do when you're in New York. I just want to see you. I want to know where you live. I want to see your bed, so I can imagine you lying there at night . . . thinking of me." His tone dropped an octave.

Just like that, her body reacted, arousal a sudden companion.

"Would you like that? You, me, this weekend? You can show me the places you like to hang out. Like, where do you get your coffee in the morning? What's in your fridge?"

She shook her head and laughed. He made it sound so simple and easy. But what stood out was that he wanted to *know* her. "Okay," she said before she could think it through.

"You won't regret it."

She smiled. "No, I don't think I will."

They made plans for him to arrive on Friday and for her to pick him up at the airport. Then he received a call, and since he was at the station, he had to take it.

She disconnected, holding the phone to her heart, which was beating hard inside her chest.

"So what's put that smile on your face?" Brad asked.

She jumped, startled. "I didn't hear you come in."

"I knocked, but the door was open, and you were lost in thought. Your hot cop?" he asked, gesturing to the telephone.

She nodded and placed her cell on her desk. She glanced at Brad, took in his *The Big Bang Theory* T-shirt with a picture of Sheldon front and center, shook her head, and groaned. "God, we need to dress you better."

He shrugged, not a care in the world. "It was the last shirt in the drawer. Guess it's time for laundry."

"You're a billionaire! Hire someone to do it for you."

"Keith likes to do it, but he was out of town on business. So what did Hot Cop want?"

She met Brad's gaze, turning serious as she told him. "He wants to come visit this weekend. And I said yes."

"You're letting someone in! This is cause for a celebration. Lunch at the Ritz. On me."

She rolled her eyes. "You don't need to make it sound like a world event."

"Oh honey, we both know it is." He settled on the side of her desk. "So . . . have you returned your mother's calls?"

"No." She twisted her hands in her lap. "I don't want to deal with her."

"Works for me. I think the less you have to do with the viper, the better."

"Well, we both know it won't last. She's relentless when she wants to be. And though she isn't happy with me, she won't leave me alone either. She still thinks she can change me."

"You mean berate you into changing," Brad muttered.

Amanda shrugged. "As long as I keep my distance, it's fine. I can handle her."

"Someone needs to cut her off at the knees."

"One day she'll go too far, and someone will." Since her therapy when she was younger, Amanda had focused on accepting herself and not changing for her intractable mother.

Brad rose. "Well, forget about her and enjoy this weekend." He leaned over and kissed her cheek.

She smiled. "I will." She was determined not to overthink things and to enjoy her time with Decklan. He knew she needed time, and as long as he respected that, things between them would be fine.

Chapter Eleven

*A*manda waited in the airport with unfamiliar feelings of excitement and longing winding their way
through her. She couldn't understand how one
man had worked his way into her head and her heart so
thoroughly, so quickly when she'd never allowed anyone in
before.

She scanned the crowd that was suddenly coming through
the gated area, when she caught sight of Decklan in a navy
T-shirt and faded jeans hugging his strong thighs. He hadn't
shaved, and the razor stubble added a dangerous edge to
the overall look. She knew the minute he caught sight of her
because his lips lifted in a sexy grin. He had a duffle bag in
one hand, and when he reached her, he dropped the bag and
grabbed her face with both hands, and soon she was kissing
him like she hadn't seen him in months instead of one week.

His lips were soft, but the kiss was anything but. He
devoured her with a hunger she matched. She grasped his
shirt and held on, reveling in the taste and scent she'd missed
so badly. His tongue slid into her mouth, and she moaned, her
fists clenching in his shirt.

"Get a room," someone called out, breaking the intensity
of the moment.

She jumped back and ducked her head, grinning at being
caught making out like a teenager.

With her cheeks burning, she met his heated gaze. "Hi," she whispered.

"Hi back."

They stared at each other, her heart growing bigger with each second that passed.

He winked, then picked up his duffel and hefted it over his shoulder. "I'm ready when you are."

"No luggage?"

"This is it."

She shrugged. "Okay, then. Let's go."

They walked through the airport and out to the parking lot where she'd left her car. She beeped the remote, and the trunk popped open.

"Nice wheels," he said of the Audi she'd purchased when Brad had threatened to sell the old clunker car she'd had since college.

She smiled. "Thanks."

They climbed into her car, and she started up the engine. Decklan watched her in silence. He didn't know what he'd expected when he arrived in DC, but Amanda's warm welcome was a solid start. That he'd managed to get her to let him come visit was a feat in and of itself, and he planned to take advantage of every minute they had together.

He glanced over at her. She wore a fitted skirt and short-sleeve blouse with killer heels. As he'd come down the escalator and through the gate, he'd been unable to take his eyes off her long legs, and the way the skirt hugged her ass, it'd taken all his restraint not to cop a feel in public.

"Did you come straight from work?" he asked.

She nodded. "It was easy enough to leave to get you by three. Brad had someplace to be, and I'd already wrapped things up for the weekend."

"Well, you look amazing." He reached over and tugged at a strand of hair that had fallen out of her messy bun.

Her cheeks flushed a hot shade of pink. He was glad she reacted to him each and every time.

"How far are we from your place?"

"Not far."

Sure enough, in a few minutes, she pulled into an apartment complex of low-rise units. A key card got them beyond a guardhouse.

"Good security," he noted.

She nodded. "It makes me feel safe. I'm more used to this kind of living than Manhattan."

"That's why I like where I live. It's not the city. I don't know how Gabe and Isabelle do it." He preferred grass and trees to sidewalks and crowds.

"To each his own, I guess."

She parked in a numbered spot, then popped the trunk so he could retrieve his bag. In silence, they walked inside. Up till now, the conversation had been benign, but he sensed her wariness. He understood that her allowing him to visit was a big deal. He respected it. But he didn't want distance between them. Not when just watching her made him hard. And as they walked up two flights instead of taking the elevator, he couldn't tear his gaze from her curvy hips, her lush ass, or her sexy sway as she moved.

By the time he stepped into her place, he caught a light floral scent, saw the sunlight bounce off her hair from a row of windows, and he was done.

But when she turned to face him, her brown eyes were wide with a hint of uncertainty, something he didn't want between them. They'd fallen into the dangerous waters of a relationship, and that scared her. She needed to feel safe with him again, and he knew just how to get her in the right frame of mind.

He dropped his bag and crooked a finger. A demand, not a question. She walked toward him in silence. Submission in the bedroom was something she understood.

And craved. And that was what he could give her, at least until she dropped the rest of her walls and let him in completely.

His being here was progress. He needed to make more.

He toed off his sneakers and stepped toward her.

"Undress me," he said.

Her eyes flashed with understanding and desire. A small grin lifting her lips, she raised his shirt, letting her soft hands touch his sides as she pulled the fabric up and over his head. Instead of tossing it to the floor, she folded it carefully and laid the T-shirt on a nearby table.

She glanced at his chest and met his gaze, a question in the chocolate depths. He nodded, and she placed both palms against the bared skin on his shoulders, searing him with her touch. Something he'd needed and denied himself for too long.

Slowly, she caressed him, making her way south. She outlined muscles he didn't know he had. Then she paused to let her fingers play with his nipples, teasing and tormenting him until his cock was rigid against his jeans, and he sucked in a sharp breath.

"Enough."

A satisfied smile lifted her lips as she began working her fingers downward. She slipped them into the waistband of his jeans, a quick tease before she undid the button, then hooked a fingertip into his boxer briefs and slid the denim over his straining erection. Pulled them down his legs. He kicked them out of the way. Once again, she bent down and retrieved his pants to fold them with care before piling them on top of his shirt.

She walked back and knelt in front of him. When she licked her lips, his heart nearly beat out of his chest. This wasn't what he'd had in mind, but it was obviously what she wanted. And when she reached out and cupped his cock in her smooth hands, he'd have given her anything she asked for.

Her grip was soft as she ran her fingers over his length. "Harder."

She nodded, but before following instructions, she leaned in and swiped her tongue along his straining shaft. The pleasure from that fleeting touch was almost enough to make him come, but she wasn't finished, making sure to lubricate him with her mouth before gripping him harder in her hand and pumping more steadily.

He swore out loud. "God, you're going to kill me," he muttered.

Big brown eyes glanced up at him, amusement and sheer desire in the depths, before she broke contact and refocused on her task. Instead of keeping up the pressure with her talented hands, she gripped his thighs and sucked him between her glistening lips.

She swirled her tongue over and around his cock, drawing him into the warm, wet recesses of her mouth. With a groan, he grasped her hair, pulling hard as he thrust in and out of her willing mouth.

Her low groan told him she liked the bite of erotic pain he'd applied. In fact, she worked at him eagerly, licking, sucking, moaning around him, the vibrations sending him to another plane of pleasure. She accepted all of him, his cock hitting the back of her throat with each pass through her lips.

He'd worry about hurting her, except she was obviously as into it as he was, her soft moans only serving to bring him closer to the brink.

Light flashed behind his eyes as pleasure and Amanda consumed him. His body drew tight, and when she swallowed around him, he was done for. He came without thought of pulling out, and considering the eager way she swallowed every last bit, he had nothing to worry about.

Except when he came to himself and glanced down, he realized her hand was beneath her skirt and she was obviously taking care of herself. Though his legs were shaking, he was still the one in control here, and she needed to know it.

He grasped her beneath her arms and pulled her up until they were nose to nose.

"What?" she asked with a too-cute pout, clearly annoyed he'd interrupted her.

"Let's get something straight."

She raised her eyebrows.

"Your orgasms are my job." He lifted her, and she wrapped her legs around his waist. "Bedroom?" he asked.

She had a pleased expression on her face, her lips turned upward in a grin, and she pointed toward the back of the apartment.

He still hadn't taken the time to really look at where she lived, and he didn't stop to do it now, striding toward the open door with one wriggling, aroused woman in his arms.

He stepped into her bedroom and deposited her on the bed. His first thought was that she had to get a king-sized mattress if he was going to stay here often. Knowing how fired up that comment would make her, he kept it to himself.

He laid her on the bed, and Amanda had never felt so wanton or decadent. She'd never had a half-naked man in her bedroom standing over her, waiting to do God knows what either. But Decklan had walked in and taken over.

And though she normally called the shots in her daily life, she loved the ability he had to make her not think. In fact, since they'd gotten together, she'd stopped focusing on herself and her issues altogether, something she hadn't realized but that dawned on her now. He really got her in a way no one had. And she was beginning to wish she could keep him without hurting Brad in the process.

The thought would have had her pulling back, but Decklan was ahead of her, as usual. "Eyes on me, baby."

She blinked and came back to focus on him.

He ran a strong hand over her calf and up her leg, his rough hands arousing her with his sensual touch. "Did I really catch you with your hand on your clit?"

She blinked up at him and smiled. "Maybe?"

He shook his head and laughed, but before she could breathe easy, he flipped her over, raised her skirt, jerked her panties down and off her legs, and treated her to one hard slap on each cheek.

She sucked in a breath at the sting, waited, and sure enough, the warmth caused her sex to tingle. "Who's in charge in the bedroom?" he asked.

She hesitated, and when he smacked her once more, she realized she'd done it on purpose, wanting this exact result. She moaned and laid her head on the bed.

"Do you plan to answer me?" he asked, running his hand over her tingling skin. "Who's in charge in the bedroom?" he asked again.

"You are." But even as she spoke, she lifted her ass up toward him, causing a low, rumbling laugh to echo from him.

"Vixen," he muttered with warmth, smacking her twice more before giving her what she really needed, his fingers inside her, his thumb on her clit, both working in tandem to give her the relief she desperately needed.

He slid in and out of her in an easy motion, and soon she was grinding against him, seeking release.

"You're so wet for me," he said gruffly.

She moaned and rubbed herself against his hand. "So close," she whimpered as the waves building inside her crested higher.

In an instant, he pulled out, leaving her empty and hanging. "Decklan!"

He lifted her hips, and she caught on quickly, bracing her arms on the mattress, raising her hips.

She felt him behind her, his warm body coming over hers. Her pussy clenched with need. She didn't care that she was still dressed, only that he could fill her and ease the empty ache he'd created.

"Now say it again."

She wrinkled her nose, though he couldn't see. "Say what?" she asked, wriggling her behind, wanting him so badly that she could barely speak.

"My name. Say my name," he muttered, sliding his fingers through her weeping sex.

"Decklan, please," she said without hesitation.

And was rewarded with the glide of his cock between her thighs. As a tease, it worked. More moisture pooled, and inner walls clenched desperately.

"Is this what you want?" he asked, his entire body covering hers, his cock lined up at her entrance.

She arched back toward him in response. That's all it took for his control to snap. He thrust so deep that she felt him everywhere. He gave her no time to prepare or catch her breath. One hand on her hip, he picked up a rough rhythm she needed as much as he did. With every drive forward, his hips hit hers and forced her forward on the bed. Only his grip held her in place. The sounds of their heavy breathing and groans mixed together. He filled her in ways she hadn't known she was empty, made her feel things she hadn't thought she was capable of feeling. He took, yes, but he gave so much more.

He'd found that spot inside her, and with every thrust and glide, she reached higher, stars, rainbows, and all sorts of fireworks building inside her, ready to go off any moment. As if he knew, he reached around and slid his fingers over her clit, adding even more stimulation to her already sensitized, ready-to-blow body.

She cried out, reaching for everything he offered.

"Come, baby, because I sure as hell am." He pulled out and plunged deep, his finger bit into her sex, and she exploded around him, her orgasm taking her higher than she'd ever been before. And even as she came, she was aware of him following her over, spilling himself inside her in the most intimate, sensual way.

She wasn't sure how much time had passed when she became aware of her breathing again or his heaviness holding her into the mattress.

In tune with her, he rolled over with a groan. "That was spectacular."

An unfamiliar feeling of warmth and pride crept over her. "Yeah?"

He gripped her face between his hands and kissed her hard on the lips. "Absolutely."

She grinned. "Well, good. And I happen to agree."

He laughed and flopped back onto the bed.

When they could both finally move, they took a shared shower, which led to her soaping him up and learning his body in ways she'd never before experienced with another man. And vice versa. He cleaned her up, helped her wash her hair, and wrapped her up in her favorite fluffy towel before wrapping one around his waist too.

Her stomach chose that moment to growl unattractively. "Sorry."

He shook his head and laughed. "No worries. I'm starving too."

"There's a great Italian place downstairs. I thought maybe we could eat there? If you want me to cook, I can do that tomorrow."

"I came here to be with you. It doesn't matter where we go or what we do."

She shook her head, grateful he was so easygoing—at least outside of the bedroom. And she was glad they could spend time together in her world too. She felt safe taking Decklan out here. She'd only recently moved to this apartment complex, and nobody knew her well enough to question whom she went to dinner with. It was only within the DC political world that Brad's father's people paid attention.

Chapter Twelve

The restaurant Amanda had chosen was a quiet one on the corner near her apartment complex. The walls were painted a pale blue, the lighting low, most of the patrons their age, people who looked like they'd just come from work and others who were dressed even more casually. Decklan felt comfortable here, with her.

They ate in easy silence. He tried the chicken piccata special; she chose the Marsala. The food was great, the company better.

"I love this place," Decklan said, glancing around while they waited for the check.

"It's relaxing. I come here a lot when I don't want to cook. Sometimes I'll bring my iPad and just read while I'm eating."

He stared at her a moment, taking in her now-makeup-free face and serious eyes and saw someone who was, at heart, a loner. Much like him. "I'm glad you let me come this weekend."

She smiled. "You were pretty insistent. But I have to admit I'm glad too."

After a shared dessert, they walked back to her apartment. As they reached the entrance to the building, a female voice called out from the parking lot. "Amanda?"

"Mother?" Amanda stiffened, then turned.

A well-dressed and very unhappy-looking woman strode up to her. "Of course it's your mother. You know, the woman whose calls you've been ignoring. The woman you kept waiting in her car?"

Amanda sucked in a sharp breath. "It's not like I was expecting you. And as for not returning your calls, I've been busy."

"Yes, working as a secretary." The older woman wrinkled her nose in disdain.

"Personal assistant," Amanda corrected her.

"Same thing."

Amanda shook her head. "Mother, please. Not again."

Since the other woman didn't seem to want to notice him, Decklan took the time to evaluate her with a lingering look. She came up lacking. Although it was obvious she and Amanda were related—blonde hair (though clearly her mother's had been touched up with a bottle), similar bone structure, and brown eye color—the similarities ended there. Where her mother was tall and too thin, Amanda was lush and curvy. Where Amanda was warm and real, her mother was full of grandeur and illusion. Or was it delusion? Decklan wondered.

"*Mother, please* what?" the older woman mimicked. "How about you show some manners and invite me inside?"

Good Lord, she was cold. How had Amanda grown up with this woman?

Amanda straightened her shoulders. But Decklan could sense how hard even that small act of defiance had been.

"Now's not a good time," Amanda said. "I have company. We just returned from dinner."

Her mother glanced at Decklan, noticing him for the first time, and her frown indicated she didn't like what she saw. Since that made two of them, he didn't much care.

"Marilyn Collins, this is Decklan Dare," Amanda said, gesturing between them.

"It's nice to meet you," he gritted out. He couldn't say it was a pleasure, but for Amanda's sake, he'd be pleasant.

Her mother glanced away from him, her eyes widening as she really looked at Amanda. "You went out to a restaurant dressed like *that?*"

She glanced down at her light-pink dress that hung gently but clung to every curve and a pair of basic flip-flops that showed off her pink-polished toes. "I like this dress," she said softly.

"It looks like you put on a few pounds too. Good thing I have a wonderful new diet. We can talk when we're alone." She pointedly stared at Decklan.

As if he would leave her alone with this evil woman.

If this was how her mother had always treated her, no wonder she had deeply ingrained self-esteem issues. There was nothing wrong with how she looked or her dress. Not a damned thing.

"For what it's worth, I think you look beautiful," Decklan said, resting his hand on the small of her back.

She didn't flinch away, accepting his show of support. In fact, she glanced up at him and smiled.

"Who are you to my daughter?" Marilyn's shrill voice captured his attention. She perched her hands on her slim hips, her annoyance clear.

So much for niceties. She hadn't even acknowledged his greeting. He wanted to shove his relationship with Amanda in this woman's face but knew better. Amanda appeared shocked, and the more her mother spoke, with her belittling tone and disgusted looks, the more Amanda quietly pulled into herself.

"We're friends," he said, hating the taste of the word on his tongue because they were so much more.

Marilyn nodded, but her eyes narrowed. Clearly she was shrewd.

"I hope that's all you are. Because I can already see your influence, and it's not good. It's bad enough she works for that . . . that man who wears T-shirts instead of a suit and tie, but at least his father is someone important. And now she's hanging out with the likes of you." She wrinkled her nose.

Decklan figured she wasn't impressed with his cargo shorts and T-shirt. Or maybe it was the razor stubble he favored on his days off. Personally, he didn't give a shit what she thought of him, but for Amanda, he cared.

"That's enough," Amanda said, her tone suddenly stronger. "There's no need to talk like that to Decklan. He's a good man, a good . . . friend, and he's a cop, which takes courage and common decency. I'd appreciate it if you'd show him respect."

He wanted to linger on the fact that she'd stumbled over the word *friends*, but instead, he was hung up on how she'd stood up to her mother for him but not for herself.

"There's no need to defend me," he told Amanda.

"Yes, there is. Come on. You don't need to listen to this." She tugged on his hand.

"You don't mean to leave me standing here, do you? I raised you better," Marilyn said.

Decklan had had enough. "Lady, if you raised her to be the way you wanted, I wouldn't want anything to do with her. Luckily, she has a mind of her own, and she's as beautiful inside as she is out."

Marilyn's eyes opened wide. "You can't talk to me like that."

"I just did."

Amanda stepped between them. "Why did you come by?" Amanda asked, resigned.

"Oh, now you care? Your father wanted you to know he was going in for a stress test next week. But I'll let him know his ungrateful daughter didn't have time to listen." And with that pronouncement, she strode toward her car, ignoring any questions Amanda asked.

Her mother shut the car door and started the engine.

Amanda turned to him, pain etched across her face. "I can't believe her. Well, I can, but still. I'm sorry you had to go through that."

"It's not me she verbally abused." Not as much as she had Amanda. "What's wrong with her?"

"Oh, that's a long story."

"One I want to hear, but let's go inside first, okay?"

She nodded, and he followed her inside and up the stairs. Once inside, she turned to him. "Listen, I'm going to change and call my dad before my mother gets back home and fills his head with more awful things about me. I'll be out in a few minutes."

"Does he have a heart condition?" Decklan asked.

She shrugged. "Not that I know of. And I figure if my mother could take the half hour to leave him and drive over here to lecture me, he must be okay, at least for now."

He inclined his head. "Go. See what's going on."

"Thanks." She headed into the bedroom.

He hated the mood and defeated tone her mother had instilled and was determined to undo the emotional damage the other woman had caused.

While he waited, he couldn't stop replaying the awful words her mother had spewed at her. Everything from her job to her dress, and worst of all, her weight—the woman hadn't had one nice thing to say. If Decklan wanted a primer on what made Amanda tick, he'd just gotten one, and it made him furious.

He heard her low voice from the other room. He shrugged and walked around the spacious apartment, taking in her home for the first time. Just as he'd expect, the place was full of warmth and personal touches. From soft, muted pastels for color, to landscapes hanging on the walls, to the occasional photograph, he felt welcomed. At home.

"Can I get you anything?" She walked back into the room, now wearing a light-gray T-shirt trimmed with aqua-blue and a matching pair of lounge pants with her bare feet peeking out.

She looked sweet and a little bit lost, and he held out his arms for her.

She didn't step toward him.

"Is your dad okay?" he asked, undeterred. He felt certain he could break through these walls.

Her expression softened. "Yeah. It's a precaution. He had chest pains. They ran some tests. It wasn't a heart attack, but they want to do a stress test and check for blockage."

He nodded. "Hopefully it'll be okay."

"Yeah." She swallowed hard. "You know, you really should get out while the getting's good. We were never supposed to be more than one night, and this is way more than you bargained for."

She started for the kitchen. He took two strides and stopped her, grasping her hand and pulling her toward the couch in the main room of the apartment. "I should punish you for assuming you know what I want, but I won't. Instead, we're going to talk."

She looked up at him, her eyes wide and uncertain. "I think I'd prefer the punishment."

He bit back a grin. "I wasn't giving you a choice."

He settled her in his lap, her curves lush and full against him. He ordered himself not to react to her body when he had to work on her mind.

"You are not going to shut down on me." He shifted her so he could see her face. "We're going to talk like adults, and you're going to tell me everything. You can start with why your mother is a raving bitch, and I'll end with showing you exactly what's wrong with everything she thinks by worshipping your body for hours. Sound good?"

She shook her head, her hair falling around her face.

"I'm not going to deny we have something good, Decklan, but I come with baggage."

"Who doesn't?"

She frowned. "My baggage feels like it could sink the Titanic."

He allowed himself a laugh at that. "Baby, your mother isn't someone I want to see often. But she's your mother. It is what it is. She's not you. And we both know she's wrong about everything she said. She just got inside your head tonight, that's all."

"You're right. I know it in here." She tapped her head. "It's harder to feel it in here." She placed her palm over her heart.

He covered it with his own. "The only one you have to please is yourself." He paused. "And me."

"Yeah, trust the dom in you to say that." Despite everything, she grinned.

"Enough stalling," he said in his best *dom* voice.

She drew a deep breath. "Do you really want the whole pathetic story?"

He brushed her cheek with his thumb. "I really do."

"Fine, but remember, you asked."

Just like she'd asked her grandmother why her mom was so mean. Amanda remembered her childhood clearly. Back then, her grandma had tried to play off her daughter's behavior.

"I was eighteen when I heard the story from my grand-mother." God, this was embarrassing. She was wrung out and just wanted it over with. "I'd had my first . . . sexual experience with a guy. It was over before it started, if you know what I mean. He wasn't even in me when he came. He blamed me. He said once he saw me naked, he just wanted it over with." She pressed her hands to her flaming cheeks.

"What an asshole," Decklan said, his hands all over her as she spoke. He slid one palm over her hair, another down her arm, always touching her, reassuring her, telling her without words that *he* wanted her.

"Yeah. Well, I can look back now and see he was probably mortified and needed to lash out. But then?" She shook her head, hating that particular memory along with so many oth-ers. "Anyway, when I got home, my mother wanted to know why I was crying. The story came out even though I knew bet-ter than to tell her. And of course, she agreed with him and started in again on all that was wrong with me."

Beneath her, Decklan stiffened. She appreciated his anger on her behalf, but she just wanted to get through the telling. And move on.

"My grandmother was staying over at the time, and when Mom went to bed, she told me how wrong Mom was—and why she was so superficial and bitter."

He waited patiently, and she went on.

"When my mother was in middle school, my grandfather lost his job, and Grandma began cleaning homes for wealthier families. My mother went to school with some of those kids. After a while, she had to wear hand-me-down clothes, and the kids at school made fun of her for it. She was angry, hurt, and turned it on the world. She blamed her parents, treated them horribly, and was determined to do better."

"I'm not feeling sorry for her," he muttered.

She grinned at that. "My mother got a scholarship to college, but she had to work part time too. But she was determined to marry well and, as Scarlett O'Hara would have said, *never wear hand-me-downs or be hungry again.* Unfortunately for her, when the guy she set her sights on brought her home, his family didn't accept her. They had plans for their son, and he was going to marry within his own social class."

"Ouch. Although, I'm thinking considering she didn't learn from how she was treated, she got what she deserved."

Amanda nodded. "She never did meet her wealthy prince. She married my dad, a nice guy from back home who sold insurance. But she was bitter. And she couldn't see the good in life or the fact that her husband provided well. He put a roof over her head and clothes on her back."

"But not designer duds," Decklan said.

Amanda shook her head. "Nope. Not until she began to max out his credit cards. And when she had a daughter, she transferred all those unfulfilled expectations to me."

"Ahh, baby, I'm sorry. You got a raw deal with her."

"There's more." She rested her head on his chest for a moment, gathering her courage to reveal the rest. "Umm . . . when I was younger, I was bulimic."

His arms squeezed her tighter, telling her without words that he was listening. He was here. And it helped that she didn't have to see his face as she revealed her deepest personal secrets.

"It started so simply, I didn't realize what was happening. My mother kept pushing me. Nothing I did was good enough. I needed better grades, better friends. I needed to lose weight, eat right. So when I was around her, I did as she asked. And then at night, I'd sneak food I bought at school because there wasn't any junk in the house. When my friends and I started to drive, it got even easier to buy and eat away from home or sneak the food into my room. I'd binge at night and throw the garbage away at school the next day. No one at home knew. Except I was gaining weight."

"Which didn't make your mother happy."

She shook her head. "She came down even harder on me because she was also frustrated, and I felt pressure to lose the weight but . . . I couldn't not eat. So I started to . . . purge. And it became a vicious cycle."

"God." His voice sounded low and raw.

Like he was hurting, for her. The thought amazed her.

"How did you stop?" he asked.

The answer to that was easy. "I got caught."

He groaned. "What did your mother do?"

She let out a laugh. "Not by my mother. A teacher walked into the school bathroom looking for someone. When I came out, she was waiting. She asked if I wanted to go to the nurse and call home because I was sick. Once again, my emotions got the best of me, and I burst into tears and revealed everything. She was so kind and wanted to help. She took me to the school psychologist."

His arms were locked around her, her head on his chest, and she found comfort in the steady beat of his heart. "I was so lucky that I found someone who really understood. And because she cared, I really wanted to please her. I wanted to get better, to like *me*."

"Did your mother know about your issues?"

"The psychologist tried to talk to her. She just said I was using any excuse to eat or get attention." She shrugged. "We had to work around her."

"What about your dad? I want to ask if he stood up for you, but given all you've told me—"

She shook her head and confirmed his thoughts. "Dad's a good guy, but Mom runs the show. She wears the pants and says jump, and he asks how high."

"I should give him a lesson or two in taking control of women."

She grinned, that thought lightening the moment. "Yeah, can we not talk about my father and . . . *that?*"

He laughed and agreed.

Her heart pounded hard in her chest, as if she'd run hard and fast and now needed to come down from the rush. To her amazement, she'd bared her soul. And he was still here, not judging. She was grateful to Decklan for that—and so much more.

Decklan didn't know how he managed to laugh after hearing about the childhood Amanda had endured. What a mess. The people who were supposed to love and protect her hadn't. She'd had no experience with a father figure who taught her about her own self-worth. *Not like Lucy, who'd had a father who thought she hung the moon and the stars,* Decklan thought.

No wonder Amanda responded to dominance like someone starved for guidance and affection. He couldn't help but marvel at her strength in coping and overcoming. Finally, all the pieces of the puzzle that was Amanda fell into place.

"Just know you deserved better," he said, wrapping one hand around the back of her neck, tipping her head, and pulling her in for a deep kiss. One that told her she was most definitely wanted, needed . . . and most definitely loved.

Yeah, he was feeling the emotion. He didn't need a dictionary to spell it out for him. Nor did he intend to do so for Amanda. For one thing, he needed time to adjust to the heady emotions and what went along with them. Not to mention the absolute stark fear that he could wake up one day and she'd be gone. After all, he'd experienced it for himself once before.

Chapter Thirteen

One month passed, during which Amanda felt like she was living a dream. One she'd never allowed herself to have. During the week, she performed a job she loved, scheduling conferences for Brad, handling his daily affairs, and joking with her best friend. And on the weekends, she saw Decklan. Either he flew to DC, or she traveled to New York. They fell into a routine, one she was beginning to believe could last—if she could delicately extricate herself from Brad's life.

She didn't know how he'd feel about them *breaking up* and him having to dodge his father's requests that he bring a date to the many functions that routinely came up for the senator and his family. And if the man ran for president, as was widely rumored—not that he'd decided, but Brad said he was close—then those events would be even more important and prominent.

But she couldn't help but feel it was time, and she didn't doubt he'd understand. She'd give him whatever leeway he needed to break the news to his father. But she needed to tell Decklan everything. There was no question she trusted him not to make the news public. And he deserved the truth.

Midweek, the telephone in the office rang, startling her out of her thoughts. "Hello, Ritter's World," she said, smiling, always amused by the company name. Bradley had refused to succumb to the mundane or anything corporate-sounding, like Ritter Software or Ritter, Inc.

"Amanda? It's Stephan Ritter."

She sat up straighter in her seat. "Senator!" She wished she'd checked caller ID before answering. "How are you?"

"How many times do I have to tell you, call me Stephan? How would it look for my future daughter-in-law to be so formal with me?" he asked.

Her hand started to shake, and her stomach accompanied it with a silent roll. "Stephan, you know you're getting ahead of yourself."

"It's just a matter of time," he said with certainty. "If my son can get his head out of his computer long enough to think straight, I'm certain it will be sooner rather than later. How are you?" he asked.

"Fine," she managed to say without choking on the word. She'd never had a problem talking to Brad's father before, but she'd never had regrets about her situation either.

"I'm just calling to ask you and Bradley to be at my fund raiser in New York on Sunday."

She glanced at the big desk calendar she kept up-to-date in case Brad wanted a quick glance. "Is this something new? Because I don't see it on the schedule."

He chuckled at that. "Yes, I have news, and I want my family there for the announcement."

"Umm . . ."

He laughed. "Let my son make use of that fancy private plane of his," Stephan said.

She and Decklan hadn't decided who would be making the trip where yet, but it looked like she'd be heading to Manhattan. "Sure. I'll let Brad know," she assured the senator.

"That's great. The family angle is an important one to the party. So wear your Sunday finest. It's at the Plaza."

She winced at the mention of his political allies.

"Okay, have to go make more calls. I'll see you this weekend." He hung up before she could reply.

She leaned back in her chair and groaned.

"Anything wrong?" Brad walked out of his office, wearing a Suicide Bunny T-shirt and a pair of faded jeans. Not an outfit his father's political cronies would approve of.

"No, but you're going to have to free up your Sunday." She pushed her chair back and rose to her feet. "I just spoke to your father. He wants us to be at an important fundraiser at the Plaza."

"Oh shit. Seriously? I promised Keith we'd go to a show on Sunday." Brad stalked to the window and looked out over the city. "Can we get out of this one?"

"It didn't sound like it. He pushed the family angle and mentioned how important it was to the party."

Well, maybe she could see Decklan before, talk to him and explain things before she made her appearance with Brad. But first she'd have to tell Brad what she was thinking.

She rubbed her temples, feeling a headache forming.

"Amanda?" Brad snapped his finger near her ear, and she jumped. "I asked if you were okay."

She'd been so lost in thought that she hadn't heard or seen him come up beside her. "Yes, but—"

Before she could continue, her phone beeped, announcing a text message, and she picked it up from her desk. Decklan's name showed above the message.

Shift change this weekend. Working. Not free till Sunday.

Her stomach twisted with disappointment. Though she'd just seen him this past weekend, every pore in her body missed him. Craved him.

Her phone beeped again.

I'll try to get off Monday so we have two days. Can you swing it?

When she didn't answer right away, her phone went off once more.

I'll show you a good time.

"That was Decklan, wasn't it?" Brad asked.

She met his gaze and nodded.

"You've seen him every weekend this past month. It's become serious."

Again, she nodded. "Brad, I have to tell him about our situation. I don't want to keep any more secrets. I hope or at least I think he'll understand."

She swallowed over the lump of fear in her throat. The fear that he'd reject her. It was so ingrained to think the people in her life would find her lacking or turn on her in some way.

Speaking of, she glanced at her best friend, whose brows were furrowed in thought. "Brad? Say something." She didn't want to lose her best friend either.

"I get it. Of course I do." He glanced toward the window, his expression sad. "Keith hasn't been happy with me or our situation."

"I'm sorry."

He shrugged. "Things were so simple at the beginning. And we were so happy. We met at a political rally, remember? I went undercover because it was a liberal, pro-gay-marriage gathering, and the senator's son couldn't be caught there."

She laughed. "I remember the baseball cap and the dark glasses. And that awful beard. Not your best look." She shook her head, unable to stop grinning at the memory.

"Yeah, well, Keith thought it was pretty funny too. One look at the guy, one conversation, and I knew what he made me feel . . . was different."

She blew out a breath. "I get that. What Decklan and I have is different too. Intense. Important." He looked at her like no one else existed or mattered. "But I won't sacrifice you. Not even for a guarantee of happily ever after." Not that Decklan was offering that. Not that she knew what he wanted. She never allowed him to say. She'd been too afraid. "I just need to put all my cards on the table. We can figure it all out afterward."

Brad placed a hand over hers. "I'm proud of you. And I need to think about doing the same thing. I know that in here." He pointed to his heart. "I'm just so afraid of screwing up all my father worked for."

"I understand. I don't want to be the one to do that either. But I do trust Decklan with our truth." Even if he didn't like what he learned, he wouldn't reveal it to anyone.

Brad pulled her into a hug. "And I trust you. You're right. We'll figure it out."

She squeezed him tight before stepping back. "You've always been there for me, the wall between me and any relationship."

Because after that humiliating mess with losing her virginity, she'd gone off to college. Met Brad. And let him be her buffer.

"If I liked someone, I wouldn't invest myself, and I'd say it was because you needed me and I would never do anything to hurt you. And I wouldn't. But Decklan pushed through my walls, and I realize now . . . I used you as an excuse not to put myself out there."

He inclined his head. "And sex in a BDSM club did the same thing. I'm almost sorry I suggested that to you. It kept you from reaching for more."

She shook her head, knowing for sure that the club had done wonders for her self-esteem. "That freed me. I needed the protection the rules provided me." And she loved the ability to get out of her own head for a while.

But Decklan was real. He was a man who'd cracked her shell and brought her to life and gave her the rules and protection when she needed it.

Another beep from her cell. She glanced down.

Make it work. I want us—just you. Me. Lots of touching involved.

Oh my God.

Decklan was offering her all of him. Her stomach curled with a whole host of emotions. Warmth, desire, gratitude, and . . . fear. Because she was about to give him the same thing. Her ultimate trust.

"Hey. Are you okay?" Brad asked.

She managed a nod, pushing back the old insecurities that rose up. Because though he was giving her what she wanted, at the heart of everything was the ingrained belief that if her own mother found her lacking, how long before any man she let into her life would do the same?

But Decklan had stood up to her mother for her. And he didn't view her as the Amanda her mother saw. No one had given her such a gift before.

She glanced at Brad. "I'm good."

He smiled, but it didn't reach his eyes. "Well, if you can find the guts to invest in a real, honest relationship, maybe I can find the *cojones* to come out of the closet."

She shook her head and groaned. "Boy, are we a pair."

"Always have been," he agreed. "And we always will be. If nothing else in this life, you and me? We're solid." He placed a kiss on her cheek.

"You're the best." She stepped back and looked at the message on her phone.

Gathering her courage, she replied.

I can be at your place Sunday around five.

His reply came immediately.

I'll be waiting.

Once Brad left the room, she sat down at her desk and realized she was shaking. Instead of letting the panic engulf her as she always did, she forced herself to think more clearly. She understood exactly where her fear came from. If she kept up this main barrier to a relationship, she remained safe. But

Amanda no longer wanted to live her life making Brad's easier so she didn't feel things. No. She wanted more of the bright colors of life that Decklan provided.

And she didn't have to look far for an example of someone who'd conquered her past. Decklan's sister-in-law, Isabelle, had a man who adored her, a baby on the way, and a career in interior design, with a boss who would be giving her leeway on working from home post baby. *A wonderful life*, Amanda thought.

But even if she allowed Decklan in all the way, there were no guarantees she'd find what Isabelle and Gabe had. Or that she wouldn't be hurt or rejected in the end.

Chapter Fourteen

Decklan kicked back in his brother and Isabelle's living room, enjoying a lazy Sunday morning. Gabe and Iz still lived in his deluxe apartment on the Upper East Side of Manhattan, but they were talking about moving to the suburbs. Decklan tried not to laugh at the thought of his brother so domesticated, because really, it suited him. At least it suited the man he was now, not the one he'd been before Isabelle.

As for Decklan, if he couldn't be with Amanda, hanging out with his family was the next best thing. Especially since Lucy had come in from LA for the weekend. She was staying with him, but she'd promised to make herself scarce later tonight when Amanda came by. Although she did insist on meeting his *new girlfriend* before disappearing. Sisters.

"What are you smirking about?" Lucy asked.

She sat cross-legged on the floor in front of a huge-screen television. Her dark hair was pulled into a messy ponytail, and she wore gray sweats. So did he. They were lounging around. There was a repeat of some television show he didn't normally watch on the screen, and he wasn't paying too much attention to the TV.

"Just thinking about you, brat."

"Ha-ha." She stuck out her tongue like when they were kids.

"Very mature. Nobody would believe you decorate the hottest nightclubs in the country."

She threw a piece of popcorn at him.

"Would you two behave?" Gabe muttered under his breath.

"You know you missed me, big brother."

He grunted in reply, and Isabelle laughed. "I can't believe how much I missed out on, growing up an only child."

"Well, you've got siblings now," Decklan assured her. In a short time, because she made his brother so happy, he'd come to think of Isabelle as his sister.

"Aww. Thanks." Isabelle blew him a kiss, and Gabe scowled. All in all, a typical family gathering.

Soon Lucy and Gabe began talking about their newest project, and Isabelle was flipping through baby books. Decklan grabbed the opportunity to change the channel. He started scanning slowly, pausing on a local station that was discussing a political fund raiser taking place in the city.

A female reporter stood outside the Plaza Hotel in Manhattan. "And Senator Stephan Ritter is about to make an announcement."

The senator was well known because over the last few months, the news media was gearing up for the presidential race with constant mentions of possible candidates. Decklan knew of the man and his ultraconservative views but didn't follow the news on the next president too closely yet. He would when the candidates were narrowed.

"Think the guy will run for president?" Gabe asked.

Decklan glanced at the screen. "That's what the pundits are saying."

"Oh, look. Here he comes," Lucy said.

The senator stepped up to a podium. He rambled a bit, and Decklan's eyes glazed over at the words. But he kept an eye on the screen, watching as the camera panned the audience for their reaction to his statement before returning and remaining focused on the silver-haired man.

"And with the blessing of my family, my wonderful wife, Nancy"—the camera captured his wife by his side—"my son, Bradley, and my soon-to-be daughter-in-law, Amanda Collins, along with my campaign manager, Mitchell Dawson, who has been with me from the beginning, as well as my loyal supporters, I hereby announce my intention to run for president of the United States."

The rest of his statement was drowned out with applause. But the camera continued to land on the people behind the senator, holding for a brief moment on a guy about Decklan's age in a suit and tie standing hand in hand with a woman Decklan would swear was *his* Amanda, dressed in a conservative yellow skirt and matching jacket, before moving on to the senator's staff.

"That looked like Amanda!" Isabelle said on a squeal, confirming what the churning in Decklan's gut already told him.

"Your Amanda?" Lucy asked.

"Shit," Decklan muttered, trying to come to terms with what he'd seen. He ran a hand through his hair, wondering if he was suddenly in the middle of a nightmare, not reality.

"Decklan? Don't jump to conclusions," Izzy said.

Gabe rose to his feet. "Well, what conclusion is there to draw other than the obvious? That she's got another life on the side? It's not like our family doesn't know about that."

Gabe referenced their father's brother, Uncle Robert, in Florida, and the fact that the man had had a wife and five children, along with a mistress with another three kids on the side. And nobody had known a thing. Not until one of his illegitimate daughters had needed bone marrow, and Robert had wanted his legitimate kids tested.

Decklan's stomach cramped. He needed information. "Where's your laptop?" he asked his brother. It was one thing not to dig up information on Amanda when they were just starting out. Now he needed more.

"I'm going to kill her," Lucy muttered, pacing the family room. "Nobody hurts my brothers without answering to me."

"Take the pit bull routine down a notch, killer," Decklan said, but he was grateful for her support.

Unlike Isabelle, who surprisingly wanted him to reserve judgment, Lucy and Gabe had jumped to the worst possible conclusion, while Decklan just felt raw. He knew what he'd seen on television, and a senator who wanted to be president wouldn't stick his neck out with anything less than facts.

Decklan was leaning toward siding with Gabe and Lucy, but he couldn't shake the fact that he'd *been* with Amanda. He'd learned about her, insecurities and all. And he'd been inside her body. He *knew* her.

Didn't he?

He was no longer certain.

Gabe had already returned from his office with his computer in hand. He opened it up, typed in his password, and handed the laptop over to Decklan. After settling into a chair, Decklan performed a quick search and turned up fascinating information on Bradley.

"It seems the almost-fiancé is—"

"You assume he's her almost-fiancé," Isabelle said, interrupting him.

Decklan turned to her. "Iz, before Gabe, your live-in boyfriend cheated on you, so forgive me if I can't trust your instinct."

"Hey, watch it," Gabe growled at him.

"It's fine. I understand what you're saying, but I have Gabe now," she said with the confidence of a woman who trusted her man. "I've seen the difference between someone who tells the truth and someone who doesn't."

Within seconds, Gabe had returned to her side and settled her on his lap. Not in the mood to watch the lovebirds, Decklan turned away and went back to the articles in front of him on the screen.

Lucy walked over and wrapped her arms around him. "I love you," she whispered.

"Love you too, brat."

"Talk to Amanda before you make any decisions," Isabelle pleaded. "I don't know her well, but I liked her. A lot."

Decklan frowned, Isabelle's words hammering home even more issues with Amanda's behavior. "She ate with my family. She went shopping with you. And all the while, she was involved with another man?"

"Maybe." Isabelle held firm.

"Call her," Lucy said, caving in a little. "See if she answers."

He shook his head. "She's supposed to be at my place by five. I'll have my answers then."

"You can wait?" his sister asked, sounding amazed.

He spun around to face her. "I have no choice. I'm a cop. I'm good at reading people." Or he'd thought he was. "I want to look into her face when I tell her what I saw. And I'll know then if she led me around by my—" He cut off his thought in deference to the women.

"I've heard the word *dick* before," Lucy said, trying to make him laugh. "I've even seen one."

Isabelle grinned.

Decklan placed his hands over his ears, and Gabe's already dark expression turned thunderous. "I don't care how old you are—you don't say those things in front of your brothers."

Both Lucy and Isabelle laughed.

"Get back to whatever you were going to say," Gabe muttered.

Decklan glanced back at the laptop screen. "Bradley Ritter's a software genius worth billions." It was the first thing that came up other than the fact that he was Senator Ritter's son.

"Could that be why she held on to him? Because he's rich?" Lucy asked.

"No," Decklan said immediately. No matter what, Amanda wasn't a gold digger. "I don't know what's going on, but that doesn't jibe with the woman I've come to know."

To his relief, no one reminded him there was every chance he didn't *know* her as well as he'd thought. He continued to read. The search turned up the basics on the senator's son. Where he'd grown up, gone to college—the same college as Amanda, which confirmed what Amanda had already told him, that she'd met her friend Bradley in college.

And when Decklan had had his brief moment of jealousy over the man she'd spoken so fondly of, Amanda hadn't reassured him. Instead, she'd panicked that Decklan was getting jealous when theirs was supposed to be a one-night stand, something fun and not serious. True, one thing they'd agreed upon from the start was that neither one of them did relationships, but Decklan had changed his mind. And he'd thought she was well on her way. Or maybe he'd just hoped he could bring her around to his way of thinking.

What a joke.

He ran a hand through his hair, frustrated. He didn't doubt that Amanda felt something for him. What he now distrusted was her integrity. No wonder the thought of something more intimate and permanent freaked her out. She was already committed to another man.

Chapter Fifteen

*A*manda ran out of the Plaza the first chance she got and grabbed a cab to Decklan's apartment. She was horrified and shocked by the senator's speech. She'd been blindsided by his public announcement naming her as his soon-to-be daughter-in-law. Brad had been taken off guard as well. Now they both had potential damage control to do with the men in their lives.

For Amanda, it no longer mattered that she'd intended to tell Decklan everything tonight, not if he already knew. She'd left Brad to deal with the congratulations and the fallout, not caring how it looked to the men in the senator's political party. Not caring about anything but getting to Decklan and hopefully revealing everything first.

The taxi dropped her off at his apartment building, and she hit the buzzer, relieved when he let her right in. By the time she reached his unit, she was out of breath and really scared in a way she couldn't put into words. Because she suddenly realized how much she had to lose.

She raised her hand to knock, when the door swung open and Decklan stood in front of her. He looked sexy in his gray sweats and white T-shirt, the muscles in his forearms bulging. His eyes lit on hers, and the dark-blue didn't glitter with anything but anger. Added to the serious look on his face, her hopes disintegrated.

"You saw the news," she said.

He inclined his head, his expression bland.

She licked her lips. "I can explain."

"This I'd like to hear," he said in a cool tone. He swept a hand through the air, gesturing for her to come inside.

She swallowed and walked in ahead of him, her grip on her handbag so tight her knuckles hurt. "Decklan, it's not what it looked like. Or even what it sounded like."

He turned, his arms folded across his chest, completely withdrawn from her. "So the senator didn't announce his candidacy for president of the United States on live television and thank his family, including his soon-to-be daughter-in-law, Amanda? And that wasn't you standing behind him in the exact same outfit?"

She laid her bag down on the sofa. "He said that. He even believes that, but it isn't true. You know it can't be true. I'm not involved with anyone but you."

She reached out to touch him, but he stepped away. "I didn't notice you or his son correcting him."

A chill rushed through her at the distance, both emotional and physical, that he put between them. It was as if the situation didn't involve him personally at all. He didn't even look at her with warmth.

Her insides trembled, and she was glad she hadn't eaten anything earlier. "I couldn't say anything. I—" She gathered her thoughts, caught her breath. "If it means anything, I planned on telling you everything tonight. I told Brad I didn't want anything between us."

"Yeah, because it bothered you so much all along?"

God, she really didn't like this cold side of him, especially when directed at her. "It wasn't my story to reveal. Decklan, Brad's gay. He's in the closet because of his father's right-wing leanings. And since I never wanted a relationship with anyone, I became his fake girlfriend. He's got a man he loves and who he can't be with. Not in public."

Decklan shook his head. "Don't ask me to feel sorry for him. He *knew* we were together, and he didn't come clean or release his hold on you and let you do it either. I call that selfish."

She shook her head in automatic denial. "He's not. He's been good to me. He was there for me." She groaned. "Look, I met him as soon as I got to college. It was right after I was hurt by the guy who took my virginity and then blamed me because he was too quick on the draw. I went away to school at my lowest, and if not for Brad's friendship, I might have spiraled back into a nasty cycle of depression and bingeing and purging. So don't feel sorry for him, but understand, please? I felt like I owed him my loyalty."

He stood up straighter, arms folded, anger clear. "And what did you owe the man you were sleeping with?"

Bull's-eye, she thought, his words stabbing her in the heart. "We were supposed to be just for fun," she whispered.

Those gorgeous eyes flashed with angry sparks. "Well, it got serious pretty damned quickly," he reminded her, shredding her with his words. "And even if it wasn't, you belong to the club. You know the rules in a D/s relationship. Honesty is important. Hell, it's important in any kind of relationship."

"Well, I don't know how to have one! And you knew that."

Her words stopped Decklan in his self-righteous tracks. His eyes narrowed as they looked at her, still glacial, but he'd flinched, letting her know she'd hit a target herself.

"Good point," he finally said.

"What?"

He stalked toward her. Not stepped. Stalked. "I said, good point. You don't know the first thing about having a real relationship." He stood so close that his body heat radiated into her, arousing her as much as the argument had.

Yep, fighting with him turned her on. She'd have to examine that another time.

"But you do understand another kind of relationship, the only kind you let yourself have for years, and you violated those rules."

She blinked at the strong, commanding tone in his voice. "I hadn't thought of it that way." But if they'd been in the club and she'd been caught lying . . . "Yes, I understand."

His eyes darkened to a stormy hue. "So you've earned a punishment."

Normally those words would excite her, but not now. Not when he was clearly still unhappy with her. He'd never been disappointed in her before, and she didn't like the feeling. It reminded her too much of the disappointment she'd been to her mother, and she wanted to withdraw into herself. But she refused to give in to the impulse. She had to stand her ground, accept responsibility, and deal with the fallout of her actions.

But she didn't like not knowing where she stood with him. The gulf between them was huge, and she didn't know how to breach it. "Decklan, I'm sorry."

"Good to know. So let's get this over with." He folded his arms across his chest. "Clothes off."

Her heart pounded so hard, she thought it would explode. She wanted him but not this way. She didn't want a club relationship with him; she wanted something real. Like what they'd been sharing before he found out about her so-called *engagement*. She wanted any punishment to be play and not because she'd let him down. But she had to earn her way back into his good graces.

Looking at his tightly drawn expression, she realized he was hurt. He needed this outlet. And she was willing to give it to him. But more than that, she wanted to learn from this. To be in this thing and fully committed. The problem with that was, she really didn't know what he wanted from her beyond making his point now.

She shrugged off her jacket, folded it and placed it on the couch, then kicked off her heels and set them out of the way.

He watched in stony silence. It was killing her. Her hands shook, but she continued to do as he'd demanded. She wriggled out of her skirt. Folded and set it on top of the jacket. Her camisole came next, and then she was standing in front of him in nothing but the tiny scrap of pale-yellow lace she'd picked out because it and the bra matched her outfit.

If she wanted to prove to him that she was sorry, that she wanted more than this, she had to get past the walls he'd erected. Because she wasn't the only one who'd risked a part of herself by getting in deeper than a one-night stand. He didn't do relationships either, but he'd committed himself to more. With her. And she'd let him down.

She clasped her hands in front of her and waited for more instruction as he stared at her dispassionately, the only indication he felt something the subtle clenching of his jaw.

Standing here so exposed and getting no reaction was worse than the first time she'd gotten naked for him. At least then he'd looked at her with yearning and desire. With warmth. He'd made her forget her struggles with her body image, which was no small feat. She'd thought she was at her most vulnerable then.

She'd been so wrong. This, now, stripped her bare inside and out.

Decklan freely admitted he'd wanted to teach Amanda a lesson. He wanted her to feel his lack of warmth and affection and understand all she'd risked by keeping something so important a secret. He also wanted an outlet for the anger that he'd built up since seeing her on that television screen and having his relationship dissected by his family. In front of them, he'd tried to act unaffected and logical, but as hours had passed, his hurt and sense of betrayal had grown. By the time she'd walked into his apartment, he'd been itching for the fight he knew was coming.

It had taken all his self-control to watch her strip for him and not touch her creamy skin. To not visibly react to seeing her reveal inch after inch of the body he adored. Her breasts were full and ripe, spilling over her bra. Her barely there panties teased him with the feminine secrets and heat hidden beneath. He wanted nothing more than to sink into her and forget that she'd kept such a big secret. That she hadn't trusted him enough to let him in. That for a few hours, he'd actually wondered if he could possibly lose her. Or if he'd never really had her at all.

He'd taken a leap by letting her in, trusting her with his heart, whether he'd verbalized it or not. He didn't do relationships either, but he'd committed himself to her. And in one minute, he'd had the illusion of happiness ripped away.

He'd experienced that once before and had promised himself never again. So yes, he had a lot of anger stored and a point to make.

Clothes removed, she clasped her hands in front of her and waited for his approval. He wasn't ready to give it.

He stared at her deliberately cold, hoping the pounding of his heart and the raw need he really felt for her didn't show. "That's not following directions. Is it? I said clothes off. All of them."

She gave him a small nod and released the back clasp of her bra, turned, and added it to the pile. His hand itched to run along her spine, to bend her to his command. To come inside her.

She slid her panties off next, placing them on the top of the stack. Then she drew her shoulders back and turned to face him.

Just as a fat tear rolled down her cheek.

"Fuck." That was the last thing he wanted and the one thing guaranteed to break through to him. He might still be angry, might still not completely trust her, but he couldn't treat her like this anymore.

He exhaled a groan. "Get dressed."

She blinked, clearly startled by the opposing order. "What?"

"I said, get dressed."

Her expression crumbled, and she turned away, pulling her clothes back on, her body shaking. Instead of releasing her from this painful scene, he'd obviously made things worse. He turned away while she dressed, gathering his emotions together. He didn't know what he felt, needed, or wanted.

He heard her sniffle, turned, and realized she was headed for the door. "Wait."

"I don't see why. I get it. I screwed things up so badly that you're done. I have no intention of dragging things out or making a scene."

"That's not what I said. Or want. I just need to wrap my head around everything." And get over the fact that she'd left out a huge part of her life as he'd revealed all of his.

"What do you want? Because other than apologizing, I'm not sure what more I can do."

She had a point. He didn't know either. Looking at her made his heart hurt. If it came down to how he felt about her in the moment, no question. He wanted her in every way he could get her. But he wanted all of her, not just the parts she chose to reveal.

He ran a hand through his hair. "I don't know."

She turned to face him. "I bared myself to you. You might doubt that now, but it's true. Just me revealing my body was like another woman exposing her soul. Same thing. So what you didn't know? It had more to do with Brad than it did with me or you." She drew a deep, shuddering breath. "I'm going to go."

He wanted to stop her . . . but he couldn't bring himself to do it. Maybe he just needed time. And clearly, she had no trouble giving it to him.

Chapter Sixteen

*A*manda flew back to DC with Brad. She refused to discuss what had happened with Decklan, and after a while, her friend stopped pushing for answers. She knew he had his own issues with Keith, and he'd let her draw into herself.

As soon as she got into the safety of her own apartment, she let herself fall apart. Sunday night, her phone rang nonstop. She didn't answer the calls, not from Brad, not from people who'd seen the news of her almost-engagement, which had been picked up nationally, and not from her mother. Marilyn had heard the news that her daughter was about to become engaged to Senator Ritter's son, the billionaire software guru, and decided her daughter was finally doing something right. She couldn't be more delighted and left Amanda many messages to that effect. The only person who never called was Decklan. Amanda ignored all the calls in favor of staying in bed.

She didn't get up for work Monday morning either. In all the years Amanda worked for Brad, she'd only taken time off when she was sick or when he forced her on vacation. So she felt perfectly validated when she called this morning and told him she wouldn't be coming in. She couldn't manage it. Couldn't get herself out of bed or rid herself of the pounding headache or the pain in her heart. A pain with Decklan's name engraved all over it.

She punched her pillow and rolled over, just as her damned phone rang. Her heart skipped a beat, reminding her of a painful lesson. Hope was a brutal companion and always let her down.

She glanced at her cell. It wasn't Decklan, and though barely twenty-four hours had passed, she'd seen his blank expression. He wouldn't be calling or texting her again.

Unfortunately, her mother wasn't giving up as easily.

"Well, she can darn well leave another message," Amanda muttered to herself.

Amanda no longer sought her mother's approval. She hadn't in years, and these phone calls only served to remind her of yet something else in her life she could never get right. She wasn't wallowing in pity; she was just facing some hard truths. Maybe she wasn't at fault with her mother because Marilyn had such high expectations, but with Decklan?

She had to own what she'd done. She'd kept something huge from him, a truth she should have admitted long before. And now he was left wondering just how they could build a relationship on a lie. And deciding they couldn't. She didn't blame him. She just wished she'd thought of things from his perspective earlier.

At first, she'd had the honest excuse that she and Decklan had agreed neither one of them wanted a relationship. And once things had changed, she'd wanted to live in the moment. She'd convinced herself that nothing that was going on with Brad meant anything in the scheme of her real life with Decklan. Because it was easier not to deal with the issue, to tell Decklan the truth, or to push Brad to change the status quo. She'd been stupid and deluded. And even selfish. As she'd told him, being in a real relationship wasn't something she had experience with. Neither was being in a functional family.

But those were also excuses. She'd screwed up. And now she was paying the price.

When her doorbell rang, she pulled her covers up higher over her head and ignored it. Of course, whoever it was wasn't giving up, but neither was she giving in. Eventually they'd go away.

Finally, there was silence. "Thank God."

"What's wrong? Do you need a doctor?" Brad asked, striding into the room.

"Oh my God, you scared the crap out of me!" She jerked up in bed and put her hand over her pounding heart.

"Have key, will enter," he said, dangling the set she'd given him for emergencies.

"This isn't an emergency," she told him. "Go away." She slid down into the bed.

"When you don't show up at work, it is one." He settled on the edge of the bed and pulled the covers away from her face. "Decklan didn't take the news well?" he asked, sympathy in his voice.

"Decklan had already seen the news." She groaned at the memory of his cold greeting and everything that had followed.

"I'm so sorry." Brad held out his arms for a hug, and she accepted the comfort, laying her head on his chest.

"He's so hurt and angry." She didn't get into the personal details of the confrontation. Those were between the two of them. "The thing is, he's not wrong."

"No, he's not. But if he knows you as well as you say he does, he'll understand you have a big heart and you were helping out a friend."

She looked up at him. "He understands that I didn't put him first. I didn't choose him over you. And you know what? He's right," she said, coming to that revelation for the first time.

She pushed herself up against the pillows and folded her arms across her chest. "If I'd seen him on television being announced as soon to be engaged to another woman, I'd not only lose my shit—I'd probably want to kill him." Looking at it that way, she was lucky he'd only had her strip before changing his mind.

As she realized how selfish and stupid she'd been, another lump formed in her throat. Both she and Brad had been selfish. "What happened with Keith?"

He settled onto the edge of her bed with a resigned sigh that didn't bode well. "He was watching because I'd given him a heads-up once I realized there'd be a press conference. And when I got home, his bags were packed."

"What? It's not like he didn't know about our charade, so why now?"

"The announcement drove the point home that we'd never have a life together. He didn't want to live that way," Brad said, his pain evident.

"God. So we both lost someone we love." She blinked, the word *love* spilling off her lips and the realization slamming into her. She loved Decklan. She wasn't sure why her emotions had taken so long to crystalize. Maybe, because like everything else in her life, she'd never felt this depth of feeling for another human being other than Brad. And that was deep friendship.

She choked back a sob. She wasn't the only one suffering.

"Is he really gone for good?" Brad asked.

Amanda shrugged as the tears came again. "I think he needs time, but I don't know if he'll ever trust me."

And once again, she was forced to admit if the situation were reversed, she didn't know if she'd be able to reextend that kind of faith and trust. Not when it had been so hard won to begin with. And it had, for both of them.

"What are you going to do?" she asked her best friend.

"I'm going to do what I should have done from the beginning. I'm going to come out to my parents and hope for the best."

Amanda blinked. "Really? You're ready for that?"

"I'm not ready to lose the man I love."

She wished he'd come to this conclusion before her life had imploded, but she couldn't tell him that. And it wouldn't change anything. "What do you think he'll say?"

"Publicly, he's opposed to homosexuality and same-sex relationships. But that's the party line. I've always known it, and I never pushed the issue." He dipped his head. "I think I've been a coward. I used his political future as an excuse."

"It's not easy, I'm sure."

"Come with me to tell him?" he asked her, placing his hand over hers.

"Of course." She wouldn't send him alone. After all, the senator might not be her father, but this was her lie too.

A few days later, Amanda found herself at the senator's newly and quickly established campaign headquarters with Brad. She'd pulled herself together after that first twenty-four hours, climbed out of bed, and returned to work. She'd promised to stand by Brad as he came out to his father, and she planned to keep her word.

They were met by Mitchell Dawson, the senator's campaign manager, a weasel of a man who Amanda had disliked the first time they'd met. Her view hadn't changed. He greeted them cordially but without warmth and escorted both her and Brad into the senator's large office . . . and stayed. He didn't excuse himself or walk out.

Amanda shot Brad a concerned look, but he shrugged. She took that to mean he'd expected the other man's presence. Mitchell was always around, even in the Ritter's personal get-togethers, silent but *there*, another reason Amanda found him creepy.

"Bradley, Amanda! So good to see you both." Stephan held Amanda's hands and kissed her cheek. "You look pale. Are you feeling okay?" he asked her.

She nodded. "I came down with something, but it's gone now." She managed a smile.

"Well, good. Bradley, take care of your girl." He patted his son on the back. "I'm sorry your mother couldn't be here too, but she's still in New York meeting with the strategists we hired."

"It's okay. I'll talk to her when she gets back. Umm . . . Dad, can we talk alone?" He inclined his head toward Mitchell, who held up the wall behind the senator's desk.

"Come on, Brad. I've known you since you were this big." Mitchell gestured to a much lower height.

Stephan glanced at Brad, who shook his head.

"Mitchell, please excuse us. Let me talk to my son and Amanda."

"But—"

The senator straightened himself to his full height. "Go, Mitchell. I'm sure you have plenty to do." He shot the other man an insistent look, forcing Mitchell to stride out, grumbling his displeasure.

He left the room but didn't close the door completely. Amanda couldn't find a way to tell Brad, so she let it go.

"Let's sit." Stephan gestured toward the couch and chairs in the corner of the office, obviously placed there for more intimate conversations.

They all settled in.

"So what's bothering you?" Stephan asked, leaning forward in his seat.

Brad reached for Amanda's hand and held on tight. "Dad, I know you think Amanda and I are going to be getting engaged. I know you love her, and so do I. But the thing is . . ."

He squeezed her hand harder. A quick glance told her he'd broken into a sweat. As difficult as he'd thought this would be, it was clearly that much worse.

She squeezed back, conveying her support.

"The thing is," he began again, "I'm gay."

"I know."

Amanda blinked, startled. *He knew?*

Brad coughed hard. "What? For how long? And why didn't you say anything?"

"Bradley—"

But Brad wasn't finished, and he went on. "Why did you not only let us perpetrate this . . . this charade, but push even harder by practically announcing our engagement on TV?" he asked, his voice rising along with his obvious frustration.

Stephan touched Brad's back. "Son, if you weren't ready to come out, it definitely wasn't my place to do it for you."

Brad turned a healthy shade of red.

"And let's face it," the senator continued, "your relationship benefited both my career and place within the party."

Amanda listened in disbelief, remaining silent, as this wasn't her family or problem.

"But your career and the party are the only reasons I didn't come out before now." Brad rose to his feet and began pacing the floor in front of the senator's big wooden desk. "I didn't want to destroy something you worked your whole life for, so I remained silent. Meanwhile, this lie has been eating me alive for years. It's put a wedge between me and the man I love, and it's cost Amanda as well."

Senator Ritter stood, and Amanda did the same. "Bradley, do not put your choices on me. I never once asked you to lie or pretend to be something you're not in order to benefit my career. You did that yourself. Admittedly, I let you, but don't mistake your choices as anyone's but your own."

Brad's shoulders slumped in silent acknowledgment of his father's words.

"I'm not saying I don't appreciate that you cared so much about me and my career. I do, and I'm grateful. But let's be clear. I didn't ask or demand it of you. I would never do that."

In that powerful reply, Amanda saw the man who would possibly one day be president. A man who was strong enough to believe in himself, selfish enough to let his son suffer without once giving him an out, and capable of twisting a situation while keeping things just on this side of the truth and coming out on top. Because the fact was, the senator had valid points. She and Brad had made their choices. And now they had to live with the consequences.

Brad ran a hand through the hair he'd styled well before coming here today. More evidence of the fraud he perpetrated in front of his father. Not that he realized it. Clearly, they both had growing up and changing to do.

"My God. I can't believe you knew." Brad's eyes were red rimmed.

The senator placed an arm around his son. "So what now? I know you came here to do more than tell me that you're gay."

Brad drew himself up straighter, owning himself and his new choice. "I want to come out publicly. I figure if Dick Cheney's daughter is a lesbian and his career survived, yours will too."

"The hell it will," Mitchell said, storming back into the room.

To her surprise, Amanda had forgotten he was listening.

"We've worked too hard to get to this point for you to blow things up at this late date." The campaign manager's face turned beet-red as he spoke.

"Mitchell, calm down. We don't live in the Middle Ages. We can deal with this. It's not like I didn't have a contingency plan all along," the senator muttered. "We will sit down with a sympathetic journalist. As a family. We'll choose someone known for the hard questions but who we can trust to give us the right spin." He was clearly in politician mode.

"Does Mom know too?" Brad asked.

The senator leveled his son with a steady look. "She raised you. What do you think?"

Amanda winced, hurting for Brad. Both his parents had denied who he really was, using the excuse that he'd never told them. But Brad's omission had been in order to protect his father, while Stephan's denial had been so he could enhance his career. Or at least not sabotage it while he was on his way up the political ladder. Still, the man seemed to accept him now, and that was a lot more than Amanda could say about her own parents.

"This is bullshit," Mitchell muttered. He picked up a glass paperweight and looked as if he was ready to throw it through the window. Or at Brad's head. Based on the way he glared at him, either was a possibility.

Stephan strode over to his best friend. "Now Mitchell, put that thing down and let's get busy. Make a list of potential interviewers. We have to find ways to mitigate the fallout."

"The only way to do that is to make sure things continue on as they were. The party isn't going to take this well. You just announced your candidacy. You bring in the heavy right-wing and Tea Party votes and money. No one will like the fact that you're embracing your *queer* son." He sneered the word.

Brad winced. Amanda was horrified.

"That's enough!" Stephan's voice boomed through the room, and Amanda stepped away, bumping into Brad. He pulled her away from both angry men.

"That's my son you're talking about," Stephan informed him. "I don't give a damn what your views are—when you speak of my family, you will do so with respect."

Despite the fact that neither man was focused on Brad himself, Amanda was, and she felt the tremor go through his body at his father's heartfelt words.

The senator and Mitchell continued to argue about the effect of Brad's orientation and the senator's plan for both the campaign and the political party he served.

"We should go," Brad said, interrupting when it became clear the other two men were going to be engaged in a long, hard battle.

Stephan nodded. "I'll be in touch with the date and time of the interview," he said, ignoring Mitchell for now. "Until that day comes, I can expect you two to carry on? Show up at any event and continue your parts?" He asked as if it were a foregone conclusion. It was.

Amanda knew she'd never turn her back on Brad or his family.

"Of course," Brad said.

Amanda managed a nod.

With Mitchell glaring at them, she turned and followed Brad out of the room, her mind spinning with all that had transpired inside. In the end, Brad had won a major battle and would probably come out with Keith by his side.

She didn't know if she could say the same of herself and Decklan.

Chapter Seventeen

*D*ue to a bout of the summer flu that had gone around the precinct, Decklan worked extended hours during the week. He was grateful for the distraction of patrol, but that didn't mean he could completely keep his mind off Amanda. And he couldn't stop replaying their confrontation over and over in his head.

She'd obviously come straight to his apartment after the senator's announcement, wanting to explain. Instead of just listening, he'd humiliated her—and he couldn't get her stricken look out of his mind. Although he wasn't the one who'd lied, he sure as hell had fucked up how he'd handled her.

His family kept calling to check in and see what had happened with Amanda, and he couldn't bring himself to admit the whole sordid mess. He could barely deal with it himself. But he wasn't ready to forgive and forget any more than he could imagine walking away for good and never seeing her again.

After his last day on patrol before a stretch of time off, he pulled back into the station lot. He parked, locked up his car, and walked inside. He had some paperwork to finish, and then he could head home. With a little luck, he was finally tired enough to sleep instead of tossing, turning, and replaying every moment in his tortured brain.

A dark-haired man sat in the chair beside his desk. He took a quick look at the man's profile and realized he had a visitor. Bradley Ritter. Although they'd never met in person and his current outfit, jeans and a T-shirt with windmills and the words "Clean Energy," was nothing like the suit and tie he'd worn on TV, Decklan still recognized Amanda's best friend.

Drawing a deep breath, Decklan stepped behind his desk, seeking the comfort of his own space before dealing with his guest.

The other man quickly rose to his feet.

"Sit down, Ritter." Decklan followed his own instruction and lowered himself into his chair.

"So no introductions are necessary," Brad said, easing back down.

Decklan shook his head. "I recognize my girlfriend's almost-fiancé." He deliberately made the first hit.

Ritter shrugged the words off. "At least you're still calling her your girlfriend."

Decklan groaned. He wasn't in the mood to spar with the man. "What do you want?"

Brad met his gaze. "So Amanda is right. You are pissed."

At the mention of her name, Decklan straightened his shoulders. He didn't like hearing that she'd discussed *them* with another man. Even if it was her gay best friend.

"I'm a lot of things, none of which I intend to discuss with you. But since you're here, I think I'll tell you a few things about *you.*"

"Go for it," Brad said.

"Fine." Decklan hadn't realized how badly he wanted this chance until now, when he was faced with the opportunity. "You may be brilliant with coding, Ritter, but I'm not sure you really understand human nature. I get that you were there for Amanda when she needed you and that she loves you." Just a friend or not, it hurt Decklan to even say those words.

He leaned forward in his seat, now on a roll. "But you took advantage of her personal issues with her parents and her desire to be loved and needed, and instead of helping her get out of her own head and meet people, you made it easy for her to hide. Because it suited *you*. Because she gave you a cover you desperately needed." Satisfied, Decklan sat back in his hard chair before finishing up with, "And that, my friend, is selfish. And cowardly."

Brad shrugged off the insult. "So is not coming out to your own family. Yeah, I get it."

Decklan blinked. Brad had just agreed with him. Decklan hadn't expected that, and it frustrated the hell out of him. How could he expend his anger at the man if he wasn't going to fight back? "What can I do for you, Ritter?" he asked again.

"I wanted to talk to you myself. And I wanted to see the man Amanda's fallen so hard for. Hell, I want to make sure *you're* worthy of her."

"Seriously? You're here to judge me?" he asked, offended since he'd been the one screwed over.

Ritter met his gaze without flinching. "As Amanda's best friend, I think I have the right. So yeah. I am. She's home crying her eyes out. She hasn't been coming into work regularly, which isn't like her. And I want to know if you're worth it."

That information wounded Decklan worse than being butted in the head with a gun. Hurting Amanda was the last thing he'd wanted. But what had he expected when he'd made her strip down, then turned her away and let her walk out the door?

He'd been so busy feeling sorry for himself that he hadn't given a thought to her feelings. Nice. He needed to get his head on straight, whatever that meant.

"That wasn't my intention," Decklan muttered.

"Well, for someone who claims to know her weaknesses so well, it seems to me you played on them yourself. She put herself out there for you, and where have you been?"

Decklan winced. Seeing it from Brad's perspective, Decklan realized he had come up as short as her best friend had. He ran a hand over his head and groaned.

"For what it's worth, I came out to my father," Brad said as he rose from his seat. "Amanda and I have to attend one last event as a couple Friday afternoon. Then my father has an interview scheduled to air that night, where he plans to reveal everything. After that, we're free. *She's* free." He treated Decklan to a deliberate pause. "It's up to you what you do about it."

Amanda and Brad flew to New York for the luncheon with the Ritter family. She arrived the day before the event and stayed the night in her rented apartment. The sadness that had engulfed her in DC followed her here. In fact, it was worse in New York, because she knew how physically close Decklan was. Ironically, he'd never been farther away.

She'd bared herself for him in all possible ways, and he'd all but sent her away. He knew she was sorry and wanted to make their relationship work. The ball was in his court, and his silence spoke volumes.

One more event for the senator and she could leave Manhattan and never come back. She promised herself that after today, she'd no longer think about horse-drawn carriage rides with the man of her dreams, orgasms that went on with no end, or erotic uses for ice cream and hot fudge.

For now, she had to focus on this luncheon. She chose a simple black-and-white dress, a pair of black pumps, and no statement jewelry. There was no need to draw attention to herself. This was a requisite photo op for the senator, and it would be the last time she'd have to play this charade in public.

It was also the first time she'd be with Brad's family since he'd come out to his father. From what Brad had told her, both his parents had taken the news in stride and were determined to make the best of their son's decision to go public with his sexual orientation. They'd deal with party politics and blow-back as it came up.

The first step in the plan was an interview with Jessica Conrad, an interviewer known for proright leanings regarding economics, but her social views were much more liberal. Knowing they would get a sympathetic ear, the senator had chosen her for their family interview.

Luckily, Amanda was excused from that particular event; however, she'd been warned to expect phone calls from the media wanting to interview her about her role as Bradley's cover. The senator had put someone in charge of handling them and deciding which, if any, interviews would be beneficial to the campaign. If they decided Amanda needed to speak, they planned to give her media training before sending her out to deal with them. She hoped like hell they decided she had nothing of value to offer the press and turned down every opportunity offered.

In the meantime, she waited for the town car hired to pick her up and take her to lunch, wondering when this feeling weighing her down would finally go away. Breakups sucked—yet another reason she was glad she'd avoided relationships for as long as she had. She didn't have to worry about future heart-break. She couldn't imagine opening her heart to anyone ever again. Never mind the fact that she couldn't picture herself feeling half as much for another man as she did for Decklan.

Lunch was an awkward event at an out-of-the-way restaurant not even Brad's mother, Nancy, a New York regular, had heard of. Apparently, Mitchell Dawson had chosen the place, claiming the donor they were wining and dining preferred his privacy. Mitchell himself was sullen and clearly still upset with the senator's plans, and he was outright cold to Brad. His silent fury, anger, and dislike emanated off the man in waves, and Amanda was grateful when he excused himself early, claiming he had a scheduled phone call he had to take.

With Mitchell gone, the mood around the table lifted, and Amanda was able to finish her meal.

Unfortunately, he met them outside the restaurant, immediately pulling the senator away for a private talk. As a good politician's wife, Brad's mother engaged the sponsor in conversation, leaving Brad and Amanda alone.

"Thanks for this last supper," Brad said.

Amanda laughed at his joke. "You're welcome. I'm glad it's almost over. I hope the interview goes smoothly for you."

He shrugged. "It'll go how it'll go. I'm not looking forward to anything but it being over. I'll deal with the media frenzy and get on with my life. What about you?"

"What about me? I'll do whatever your father needs with the press. I'll be at work. I'm not going to let my professional life fall apart just because my personal one did. I'm sorry I flaked out on you this week."

Brad frowned. "Don't apologize. I put you in a horrible position and should have ended this charade years ago."

She wrinkled her nose. "What are you talking about? This worked out for us both, at least until recently. It was a mutually beneficial arrangement."

He grasped her hand. "Decklan was right. It was a selfish arrangement and—"

"Wait. You spoke to Decklan? When?"

A loud crack rent the air before Brad could answer. Amanda screamed as blood blossomed on Brad's chest, and his face froze in terror. He grabbed his shirt, and a rush of red fluid immediately oozed through his fingers, snapping Amanda out of her shock.

"Oh my God!" she screamed. "Brad! Help! He's been shot!" She dropped him to his side, unsure of what to do. How to stop the bleeding. She pressed her hands on top of his, a sob catching in her throat as her fingers turned scarlet and wet.

Nancy shot to her son's side, pressing her hands over Amanda's. "Call 911!"

Shaking, Amanda slid her slick hands from beneath Nancy's. She wiped her hands down her dress and retrieved her cell. All the while, his mother spoke to him, her voice soothing and calm, begging him to keep his eyes open. To remain conscious.

Amanda's vision blurred as she dialed, and she shook while she waited for an answer. From the corner of her eye, she saw that Mitchell had pushed the senator down, covering his body with his own.

The minute the dispatcher answered, Amanda focused on answering the questions the operator asked. After what seemed like the longest minutes in history, the wail of an ambulance finally broke through the madness around her.

"Thank God."

Chapter Eighteen

ecklan had asked Max to meet him at the club. He hadn't been to the place since the last time he'd met up with Amanda there. He hadn't missed it either. But he couldn't help but admit it felt good to be here now, nursing a soda and waiting for his best friend. Especially when he'd come to a decision about Amanda and he had time to kill before he could do anything about it. He didn't want alcohol dulling his senses when he dealt with Amanda later on.

Because it was daytime, there wasn't any play going on, just a few members having a drink or meeting to talk. A big-screen TV hung above the bar, playing the news, and Decklan kept an eye on the closed captions while waiting for Max.

"Good to see you," Max said, joining him at their favorite seats by the bar. "So what's the deal with Amanda? You two back together yet?"

Max knew the bare-bones details about Amanda's fake relationship with Brad. He knew nothing about their interaction after, specifically Decklan's behavior. Decklan had always known that no matter what he decided about the future with Amanda, he owed her an apology for preying on her weakness. *That* hadn't been his intention.

"Not yet. I'm going to go talk to her in a little while. She's got one last required event with the Ritters." Then, to quote

Brad, she was free. And once there were no external barriers keeping them apart, he intended to make things right.

"And then you're going to get your girl?" Max asked.

"That's the plan."

"Does she want to be gotten?" he asked, laughing.

Decklan groaned. "That's the big question. I fucked up."

Max leaned an arm on the bar, studying him with too-knowing eyes. "Well, no shit, buddy. You're you. You have abandonment issues."

Decklan rolled his eyes. "Why didn't you become a shrink? Then you could spend your days analyzing everyone else's problems, and you'd be too sick of it to bother with mine."

Max grinned. "Because my father left me his business, that's why. Now let's get back to you."

"Okay, Freud. I had a visit from her best friend. The senator's son. I gave him a piece of my mind, but in a few succinct words, he let me know I hadn't handled things with her any better."

After signaling for a drink, Max turned his attention back to him. "Spell it out."

"Instead of accepting her explanation and apology, I basically stripped her of her defenses, got pissed at myself, and sent her on her way." The memories of that night were still crystal clear and just as painful now as then.

Max shook his head and let out a low whistle. "Because you'd rather push her away than lose her some other way. Like I said, abandonment issues."

"Go away."

He shrugged. "Hey, if the shoe fits . . ."

It did. Too well. Decklan just hadn't viewed things from that perspective. Sometimes Dr. Freud had good points, not that Decklan would tell him and give him any more of a swelled head.

But the gut-wrenching truth was he'd taken a woman who was just waiting for everyone in her life to find her lacking, and he'd done just that.

"Shit, man. Look." Max pointed to the television screen.

Decklan glanced up, and his heart practically stopped beating as he read the closed-captioned words on the screen, *Presidential candidate Senator Stephan Ritter and family involved in shooting downtown.*

"Hey, turn the volume up," Max yelled to the bartender.

The man did as Max asked, and bits and pieces of the report filtered through to Decklan.

The senator or a member of his immediate family might have been shot, according to witnesses from inside the restaurant . . . Information is sketchy at this time but . . . taken to Mt. Sinai Hospital.

Spots flashed in front of Decklan's eyes, and his brother Gabe's voice sounded from inside his own head as long-buried memories rose to the surface. *Mom and Dad were in an accident . . . eighteen-wheeler . . . the car rolled . . . no survivors. Mom and Dad didn't make it.*

Decklan knew he wasn't that kid again, but Amanda had been with Brad at the event, and there'd been a shooting, and someone had been taken to the hospital. He couldn't live through that kind of loss again. He just couldn't.

Suddenly Decklan felt himself being shaken hard, and he refocused on the dark club walls and his best friend in front of him. "Come on. I'll get us a cab to the hospital," Max said.

But Decklan remained frozen in his seat.

"Hey, buddy. You okay?" Max asked with true concern in his voice.

When Decklan didn't answer, Max handed him his cell phone, which he'd left lying on the bar. "Call her. Make sure she's okay."

He didn't know what he'd do if she wasn't. All this time spent angry and hurt, when they could have worked through things together. Now if she'd been hurt, if she was killed . . . His stomach rolled at the thought.

"Decklan, dial the damned phone, or I'm going to beat the shit out of you in order to bring you back to the here and now. Snap out of it," Max demanded loudly.

To his shock, Decklan burst out laughing. "You did not just use your dom voice on me."

"Thank God you're back."

Decklan pulled up Amanda from his favorites and hit send on his phone, but it went straight to voice mail. His insides felt like ice, but he pushed forward. He already knew what it was like to live without Amanda in his life for a short period of time. Being separated by death just wasn't an option. So as the taxi headed for the hospital, Decklan prayed fate wasn't going to shit on him a second time and rip someone he loved away from him.

The cab dropped them off at the emergency room entrance. Decklan left Max to pay. The media had already begun to set up camp outside the hospital, but in the chaos, Decklan was able to slip through the main doors and into the waiting room.

Heart pounding a mile a minute, he found the desk and braced both hands on the counter. "I need to know if Amanda Collins was the shooting victim."

"Are you family?" the older woman in charge asked. "Because we can only reveal patient information to family."

Decklan clenched his hands into fists in frustration. "Look—" He reached for his badge, determined to use any means necessary to get inside.

"Cardiac emergency!" paramedics called out as they rushed in, carrying a man on a stretcher and heading through a set of double doors.

The woman behind the desk jumped up, forgetting all about Decklan, obviously rushing to help organize things inside.

Max glanced at him. "What's up?"

Decklan shrugged. "They won't tell me anything." But the Nazi behind the desk was gone for now. "I'm going in."

He walked straight through the same double doors the paramedics had used seconds before. He was immediately engulfed in chaos, no doubt thanks to the current emergency and the fact that someone in the senator's family had been shot.

He scanned the room and saw the senator. So he was okay. Decklan kept going, his gaze hitting on the senator's wife, who had blood all over her clothes and was crying and being comforted by her husband. No sign of Brad. Or Amanda.

His hands were sweating badly, and panic threatened to engulf him.

"It's not her," Max said, putting a solid hand on Decklan's shoulder.

He hadn't realized his friend had followed him inside. "How do you know?" he asked, hope building inside him.

Max shrugged. "I charmed a nurse, how do you think? It's the senator's son, Brad. He was hit."

Decklan's knees nearly buckled. He wasn't relieved Brad had taken a bullet, just that it wasn't Amanda. "How bad?"

"No news yet. He's in surgery to have it removed."

Decklan glanced around. "Then where's Amanda?"

"In a cubicle. She was hysterical, and they had to sedate her. Apparently she was there. Had her hands on his fucking chest, Deck. She's in three." He pointed to an area cordoned off by a blue curtain.

Decklan brushed past Max and made his way to the cubicle, ignoring a nurse who tried to stop him with her nagging voice.

He pushed open the curtain and stepped inside. Amanda lay still in a propped-up hospital bed. Blood covered her black-and-white dress, an eerie scarlet spattered all over. Her arms held blood traces as well. He knew she'd want that gone as soon as possible.

He stepped over to the bed. She didn't stir.

"Sir, you're going to have to leave." A nurse walked up behind him.

"The hell I am. She needs someone here when she wakes up. Would you want to come to alone in a cold hospital covered in your best friend's blood?" he asked the woman.

She opened her mouth.

"I thought not," he said, not letting her speak. "I'll call you when she wakes up." He turned away from her, ending the discussion, as far as he was concerned.

"I'll be right outside," she told him.

He refocused on the woman lying so quietly and said a prayer of thanks. He hadn't prayed since he was a kid, but he did so now, knowing he was lucky. That he'd let his own fear and maybe even his ego get the better of him. If he'd lost her without ever telling her he loved her, he never would've forgiven himself.

He wasn't about to live in fear anymore. And he wasn't about to live without Amanda. So he pulled a chair up beside the bed, lifted her hand in his, and settled in to wait until she came to.

Amanda woke up, and the first thing she noticed was a bright light overhead. She blinked, and immediate memories came flooding back. The hot summer air, the sidewalk outside the restaurant, the sound of a gunshot, and Brad's blood. So much blood.

She struggled to sit up, intending to look for him, but dizziness assaulted her, and she fell back against the uncomfortable bed.

"Easy." A strong hand came to rest on her shoulder.

"Decklan?" She turned toward him, surprised to see him here, and wondered if she was hallucinating.

"I need to let the nurse know you're awake." He squeezed her hand and started to rise.

"Wait. How's Brad? Is he . . ." She couldn't get the last image of him out of her head and swallowed over a sob.

"He's going to be fine," Decklan said in a soothing voice. "And you need to stay calm, or that nurse is going to give you another sedative."

She swallowed hard, her mouth and throat dry. "I lost it. The ambulance left with Brad. His mom went with him. The senator took me with him to the hospital. We got here at the same time as the police. They wanted answers. I looked down at my hands, and there was blood everywhere. No one would tell me how Brad was, and I got hysterical." She ducked her head in embarrassment.

"A form of post-traumatic stress." A nurse with black hair pulled back, who looked to be in her midfifties, walked over to her. "I heard voices. You're awake, which is good. Your friend here is right. Stay calm. You don't want us to have to sedate you again."

"Okay."

The woman took Amanda's blood pressure and temperature while Decklan hovered. "All normal." She smiled. "I'll bring you something to drink, and you should be out of here soon. But the police have been waiting to talk to you." The nurse, all brisk efficiency, strode out of the room.

"Do they know who . . . shot Brad?" she stumbled over the words as she asked Decklan.

He met her gaze and shook his head. "Frankly, I had to sneak in here to see you. I wasn't about to risk being thrown out by wandering around out there."

"Luckily for you, I'm braver than he is," Max said, pushing back the curtain and walking in. "I've been so busy making myself useful bringing people food and drinks from the cafeteria, no one thought to ask who I was or throw me out. I've got as much of the story as I could overhear from listening in on the senator's family."

Amanda shook her head and laughed. She glanced at Decklan to see his lips turned upward in an almost-grin. Even he found his friend amusing.

As much as she wanted to know why Decklan was here and what it really meant, she was desperate for information about the shooting too. "Tell me what you know," she said to Max.

He braced a hand on the rail at the end of the bed. "From what I can gather, and it isn't much, they have a guy in custody.

They also picked up the senator's campaign manager for questioning. No one's saying why."

Amanda shivered. "He always scared me."

Decklan ran his fingers back and forth over her hand. She wondered if he realized he was doing it or just how soothing she found his touch. It was driving her crazy, not knowing what had brought him here—or if he planned to stay.

"We'll know more when the cops talk to the press or release a statement," Decklan reassured her.

Max nodded. "And now that I know you're okay, I'll leave you two alone. Make the most of the time you've got, because the cops will come in to question you any minute." He shot Decklan a pointed glance, then stepped over to Amanda and kissed her cheek. "Let him take care of you, doll."

Max straightened and walked out, leaving Decklan and Amanda alone.

Chapter Nineteen

Decklan never got the chance to talk to Amanda. As soon as Max left, the cops came in to take her statement. Knowing her story was necessary and he wouldn't be getting her alone unless she spoke to the police, he resigned himself to waiting. Though the officer in charge asked him to step outside, Amanda insisted he not leave her alone—not that he'd had any intention of walking away. Not ever again.

She answered question after question, her voice trembling, her face pale as she recounted the event, until she looked ready to pass out. Decklan ground his teeth through the entire telling, her fear and panic becoming his as he realized how close she'd been to the bullet that had hit her friend. And all he could do was place a hand on her shoulder and listen. He'd never felt more useless in his life.

Finally, the cop had enough. He told her he'd be in touch if he had more questions. She was drained and exhausted, and the last thing Decklan wanted was to force her to have another emotional conversation with him.

She had to go through another check of her vitals and a talk with a doctor and a social worker about post-traumatic stress and what to expect once she left the hospital. Decklan doubted she processed anything they told her, but he did. And he intended to make sure she knew she wasn't on her own in dealing with this. Anything that affected her affected him, and he would make sure she knew it.

The doctor signed her out, and then she insisted on checking in with Brad's family. They were warm and kind to her, worried about her welfare as they assured her that Brad was in recovery now and would eventually be fine.

She was swaying on her feet, and Decklan had had enough. "Time to go home. You need to rest."

She shook her head, an obstinate look on her face. "I want to wait until Brad's in a room and can have visitors. I need to see for myself that he's okay." She glanced up at him with those big brown eyes he normally couldn't resist.

He steeled himself against her appeal. If she wasn't going to look out for herself, he'd just have to do it for her. "You can come back tomorrow when Brad's more awake and you've had some sleep. You're dead on your feet."

"But—"

He grasped her arm and led her away from Brad's family. "Do you really want Brad to see you covered in his blood?" he asked, his tone deliberately gentle but firm.

She opened her mouth, then snapped it shut again. "Fine. You win."

"It wasn't a contest."

He would have picked her up and carried her out, but he didn't trust her not to make a scene. And it would only be making *him* feel better to have her in his arms. She was still hurt and angry with him, and he didn't blame her.

At least she was accepting his support, and right now, he'd take what little he could get.

His hand on her back, he led her out of the hospital and into the hot summer air.

She stopped at the curb and turned to him. "I can take a cab to my apartment from here." Before he could ask what apartment, she explained. "Brad rents one for me for when we're in the city."

A new piece of information. Apparently they had catching up to do about parts of her life he knew nothing about.

"You'll come home with me," he insisted.

"Why?" She straightened her shoulders and met his gaze without flinching. "Why are you here, and why do you want me back at your place?"

He groaned. "Listen, it's hot as hell, and you need to be in air conditioning. So let me just get you back to my apartment, and we'll talk there." He took her silence as approval and flagged down the nearest empty taxi.

He didn't relax until they were out of Manhattan and the cab driver had dropped them off at his place in Great Neck, and they walked inside his apartment. Just knowing he had her here gave him hope that they could get past their last awkward time together.

"I know you want to talk, and so do I. But can we get you cleaned up first?" he asked.

Amanda nodded, sudden tears in her eyes that she swiped with one hand. "I don't know what's wrong with me. I'm never so emotional."

"It's the adrenaline drop. You've had a huge shock today. You went through something not many people ever experience. Remember what they told you at the hospital? Everyone's reaction is different but to expect yourself to be emotional."

She nodded. "I think I'd like a shower."

He followed her into the room. While she headed for the bathroom and he heard the sound of the shower running, he pulled out a pair of old drawstring sweats and a T-shirt.

She'd left the bathroom door open, so he walked inside and placed the clothes on the bathroom counter.

A quick glance at her and he realized she was staring down at her bloodstained dress, tears dripping from her eyes and her hands hanging uselessly at her sides.

"Come on. Let me help."

She turned toward him, and everything he felt for her washed over him in one never-ending wave. Heart lodged in his throat, he took over, wiping her tears with the towel, then helping her out of her clothes. She moved slowly, and he didn't push. Nor did he let his gaze linger on her body as she stepped out of her undergarments. She was so fragile at that moment that he wanted nothing more than to gather her in his arms, but he sensed she still wasn't ready.

Instead, he turned away as she stepped into the shower, and knowing she wouldn't want any reminders of today, he balled the garment up and tossed it into the trash.

"I'll wait outside," he said loudly over the sound of the running water, prepared to give her privacy.

But when his answer was a gulping sob, he turned back around to find her leaning against the shower wall, her shoulders shaking.

"Fuck it," he muttered and quickly stripped off his clothes, opened the shower door, and stepped in to join her.

Amanda didn't know why, but as soon as she hit the shower and saw the first bit of blood run from her arms to the floor, she fell apart, and Decklan was there.

He pulled her into his arms. "Let it go," he urged.

And she did. She wrapped herself around him, his solid body her safe haven as she fell apart completely.

She came back to herself in slow bits of awareness. Decklan's big hands caressing her back, his deep voice whispering in her ear, warm water cascading over her as she curled into him.

She pulled back. "I'm sorry."

"Don't be." He gazed at her, intense dark eyes looking right into her soul. "Are you okay?"

She nodded. "I am now."

She soaped herself up, more capable now that the hysteria had passed. She felt much better once all the evidence of today had swirled down the drain. She quickly handled her hair, using shampoo and conditioner she'd left here and that he hadn't gotten rid of.

Interesting.

So was his showing up at the hospital.

She tipped her face up to the water, and hopefully she rid herself of the worst of the makeup mess she was sure to have had covering her.

He looked at her. Smiled. Then reached out, wiping beneath her eyes with his thumbs.

His touch was so sweet. Familiar. *Needed.*

"Decklan, what are we doing?" There was no mistaking what she meant.

They were both naked in the shower, two people who hadn't spoken in too long, and the last time had been hurtful and ugly. But she didn't feel any of those emotions now. She just felt taken care of and . . . loved. She swallowed hard, the lump rising in her throat because she wanted that last one to be true.

He braced his hands on either side of her face. "We're doing what we should have been doing all along. Being together. Believing in each other. Being there no matter what."

"But I lied—"

"And I screwed up how I handled it after I found out. I have no good excuse except—"

She placed her finger over his lips. "I don't care about why. I just care that you came around. I shouldn't have kept something so important from you."

"And I have issues stemming from losing my parents in such a traumatic way. We were getting so close . . ."

"You pushed me away first?" She rose to her tiptoes and briefly pressed her lips against his. "Can we agree to forgive and forget?"

"We can." He grinned. "Now can we get the hell out of this shower? I'm turning into a prune."

She laughed and nodded. No sooner had she stepped out and dried herself off than Decklan picked her up and carried her to bed.

"I'm not finished with you yet," he said in that deep, commanding voice she loved.

"No?"

He came over her, his naked body covering hers, and she moaned, soaking up his strength and body heat. "No."

She raised her arms, intending to grip the headboard, hoping he would take her body to miraculous heights, when he surprised her.

He slid his hands into hers. "Touch me."

She felt the smile pull at her lips. She'd been waiting for this moment since the night they'd first been together. "Really?"

"Really. Ask me why."

"Why can I touch you?" she asked, finally running her hands over his well-honed body and enjoying every touch, every caress. She could finally show him she cared, and she reveled in that fact, knowing she'd never get tired of touching him.

He braced his arms on either side of her shoulders and began to rock his body over hers, the hard length of his erection gliding over her sex. She moaned, arching up and into him, her body clenching and craving his.

"Because I love you, Amanda. You can touch me any way you want, any time you want, because I love you."

She opened her eyes and met his gaze, his expression full of emotion. For her.

Her heart filled. "I love you too."

He shifted his lips, lifted himself up, and slid into her in reply. She sighed in pleasure, amazed at how full she felt, not just her body but her heart. She curled her fingers around his biceps, as he didn't thrust hard, just rolled his hips, pushing into her, making love to her in the sweetest way possible.

She knew there would be times he would want it harder, need to tie her up or have her submit, and she'd need those moments just as much. But now? As he took her up and over, he completed her, and she knew she'd come home.

Amanda hung up the phone. She was smiling so wide, her face hurt.

"I take it that was Brad?"

She nodded. "He's in his own room. Recovering. Keith is hovering over him, which he loves. And though his parents met him under the worst of circumstances, I think the life-or-death thing showed them what was important. The senator accepted their relationship. He actually wished them well."

Decklan raised his eyebrows. "That's amazing for them."

"Miracles happen." She stepped into his waiting arms and rested her head against his chest, savoring the steady beat of his heart.

"Did he say if the police know anything?" Decklan asked.

She stepped out of his embrace and walked to the kitchen, then poured them each a cup of coffee she'd set to brew earlier. "The guy who shot Brad was detained by witnesses." She added milk and sugar to hers, milk only to Decklan's, and handed him his.

"Thanks."

She nodded. "Faced with being arrested, the shooter sang like a canary. The senator's campaign manager hired the guy." She shivered at the thought. "I never liked the man. He always gave me the creeps. And I knew he wasn't happy when he found out the senator planned to go public, but this?" She shook her head.

"Sick bastard," Decklan muttered.

"Yep. He wanted Brad out of the picture before his homosexuality was exposed and the senator's campaign took a hit."

"How the hell did he think he'd get away with it?"

"He figured if he could hire a guy and make it look like a random crime, he'd build sympathy for the presidential candidate whose son was killed." She took a sip of much-needed caffeine. "The senator believes the Second Amendment gives the average citizen the right to bear arms, so his manager planned to push him toward major speeches where he'd say,

'If my son was armed, he would still be here today.' Play the sympathy angle."

Decklan shook his head. "Has he lost his mind?"

"I'm not sure he ever had it," Amanda said. "The bottom line is, he just wanted Brad gone. And he almost got his wish." Her voice shook at the very thought.

"Well, he didn't. Do you want to get ready to go to the hospital and visit?"

She nodded. "But we have to stop by my apartment so I can pick up a change of clothes. I think I'd call too much attention to myself in your sweats and my high heels."

He grinned. "You look hot in anything."

She stepped back and patted his cheek. "Charmer." She started for the bedroom, but he grabbed her wrist.

"I have a question."

She spun back around, happier than she'd been in . . . ever. Not only did she have Decklan back, but there were no more lies between them. "The mood I'm in, I'm likely to agree to anything." She wiggled her eyebrows seductively. "Go on. Ask."

"Would you move to New York? I know you'd have to give up your dream job, but with Brad's reference, I'm sure you could find something flexible here. And let's face it, Gabe is pretty influential himself. He could help."

The only sign he felt unsure of himself was the muscle ticking above one eye. "Good thing I thought about this."

"Seriously? When?"

"Last night, while I laid in your arms, I knew I couldn't be without you anymore. And Brad, well, after what he's been through, he'll understand needing to be with the one I love."

"Damn, that was easier than I expected." He grinned, lifted her up, and spun her around before walking back toward the bedroom.

She squealed and grasped him around the neck. "What are you doing?"

"Taking you to bed." He had her down, clothes off, and cuffed to the bed before she could blink. She immediately became hot and aroused.

"Glad to see some things don't change." Decklan laughed. "I'll always want a little kink. How about you?"

"Always," she said in a soft purr, her body already softening for him. Not her nipples—those were tight peaks. "What about the hospital visit?" she asked in a needy voice.

"We'll get there. I promise. I just want to celebrate." He pulled his shirt over his head, giving her a good look at his gorgeous, tanned skin and muscles she'd felt over and over last night.

"What are we celebrating?" she asked, rolling her hips in a blatant bid for attention.

His eyes dilated. "We're celebrating forever, baby. That's what we're celebrating."

And that was perfectly fine with her.

NY Dares Series continues with . . .
Dare to Seduce, Book #3

NY Dares Series
Book 1: *Dare to Surrender* (Gabe & Isabelle)
Book 2: *Dare to Submit* (Decklan & Amanda)
Book 3: *Dare to Seduce* (Max & Lucy)

Turn the page to start reading the *Dare to Seduce* excerpt!

Chapter One

Max Savage glanced across the lush green lawn of Gabriel and Isabelle Dare's Bedford, New York, home, his gaze focused on the sexy brunette he couldn't get out of his head. Lucy Dare, dressed in a conservative pantsuit, her luxurious dark hair pulled into a bun, stood beside her date, a Hollywood director who was a douchebag of the first order.

The last time Max had seen Lucy, she'd been her wild and free self. Then she'd hooked up with that guy, and she'd changed. And not in a good way. He wanted fun, sexy Lucy back.

"How badly do you want to punch that guy's teeth in?"

"So badly," Max muttered, then glanced over, realizing the question came from Lucy's brother, Decklan Dare.

Max shook his head and changed his answer, because it would do no good to let his best friend know he was obsessing over the guy's little sister. He'd kept it to himself for years, partially as an excuse to deny what he really wanted, but regardless, this wasn't the right time to bring up the issue.

"Who do you mean?" Max asked.

Decklan rolled his eyes. "Oh, come on. I know you hate that Spielberg wannabe as much as we do."

"Can't say he'd be my first choice for your sister."

159

"That's rich, considering it's your fault she's with him to begin with." Decklan eyed Max with distinct annoyance in his gaze.

"How the hell do you figure *that?*" Max asked.

Decklan's older brother, Gabe, joined them, and from the look on his face, he'd clearly caught the tail end of the conversation.

"Face it, Savage. We know you have a thing for Lucy," Gabe said.

Just how the brothers had gleaned that bit of knowledge was beyond Max. Nobody had a better poker face than him.

Decklan merely nodded in agreement.

"You didn't take your chance last time she was in town, and now she's with that asshole," Gabe added, angling his head toward where his sister stood with Lucas Kellan.

"Well, fuck." Max wasn't about to deny what had clearly been more obvious than he'd intended.

Both Dare brothers narrowed their gazes on him, waiting for an explanation.

"What? I didn't think you'd approve, and I wasn't about to mess up years' worth of friendship if you didn't." He was sticking to the tried-and-true excuse he'd told himself for years. In reality, Max had his reasons for staying away from Lucy for so long and for fucking up more than just his life in the process. But they were his, and he wouldn't be sharing them.

"The only way you'd compromise friendships would be if you used or hurt my sister. If your intentions are honorable, I have no issue," said Gabe, the man who'd raised Lucy after their parents died in a car accident.

Max glanced at Decklan. They both knew Max's recent past. He'd married young, lost his wife, Cindy, in a car accident, and had a subsequent lack of serious relationships since. What Decklan didn't know was the guilt Max harbored over the emotions he hadn't been able to give his wife, due to the feelings he'd always had for Lucy. Hell, he'd married Cindy because he didn't have those intense feelings, and everyone had paid a price.

Max shifted uncomfortably and cleared his throat and glanced at Decklan, who, like Gabe, was extremely protective of his sister. "You too? You're okay with this?" he asked.

His best friend shrugged. "Well, you're an asshole, but you're our asshole." He slapped Max on the back, his expression sobering. "Look, Cindy died four years ago, and you haven't been with anyone seriously since."

Neither one of them mentioned Max's penchant for sex clubs on the weekends. It had been a way to fill the emptiness inside him, nothing more.

"But Gabe is right," Decklan said. "I see how you look at Lucy. You should do something about it if your intentions are solid."

They finally were. For years, Max had denied his need for Lucy and the emotional bond he knew they would share if they took things to the next level. Fear had driven him. Now Max was finally ready to go after the woman he'd always wanted.

"Just don't blow it, or we will have an issue," Decklan cheerfully added.

Max didn't need to be told twice. He made his way across the lawn and veered between guests, coming up to where Lucy and her date stood by the bar. Before he could interrupt, he caught their conversation.

"I hope we don't need to stay much longer." Lucas glanced at the ostentatious gold watch on his wrist, his impatience obvious. "I have calls to make, so I'd like to get back to the hotel soon."

Lucy's eyes opened wide. "It's my brother's engagement party! I'm staying until the end. Longer, even, so I can spend time with my family."

Lucas ran a hand over the top of his stylishly cut blond hair. Looked like Lucy had a type, too. Not that Max thought he had anything more in common with the director than hair color.

"Come on, babe. You live in LA, and your brothers are way across the country here in New York, so how much do you really want to spend time with them? We've been here an hour. I say we're good to go," Lucas said, cementing Max's gut feeling. The man was an uncaring ass.

What kind of asshole got between a woman and her family? Max wondered, curling his hands into tight fists. And how could Lucy be with the bastard if he didn't understand what her brothers meant to her and why?

Her pretty eyes filled with angry, frustrated tears. "You leave then. I want to be here."

Lucas studied her face for a beat, clearly assessing whether she was serious. "Fine, we'll stay." He didn't sound gracious about the concession. "But I'm going to need to make a few calls from the car. Okay?" Before she could answer, he nodded. "Okay." He had the gall to wink at her, then leaned over and placed a quick peck on her lips.

Max's fists grew tighter. Part of him was disgusted by the other man's mouth on hers; another knew a woman like Lucy deserved more than that pathetic excuse for a kiss. If she belonged to him, he'd seal his lips over hers and thoroughly devour her luscious mouth. He'd make sure his tongue swiped through the deep recesses of her mouth so his taste lingered inside her long after they parted. And he'd damn well ensure that he left her lips puffy and well kissed, so no other man would try to make a move on his female.

Caveman mentality? Maybe. But those were the feelings Lucy Dare stirred inside him.

Instead of waiting until lover boy walked away, Max strode over and slid an arm around her waist. "Hey, princess." He'd been calling her that since she'd turned sixteen and spent the day wearing a crown. As she'd grown up, the nickname had stuck.

"Max! I didn't see you arrive," she said, startled.

"Business meeting. I ran late," he explained.

"And I want to hear all about the newest restaurant you're planning and which chef you've managed to lure away from which pissed-off restaurateur."

Max grinned, excited to share the details with her. Very few knew about his plans. He was waiting to do a press release and promo op with his choice.

"You know me well." Since her boyfriend was busy glancing at his phone, Max cleared his throat and said, "Aren't you going to introduce us?"

Lucy blushed. "Max Savage, this is—"

"Lucas Kellan," the other man said, shaking Max's hand in a limp grip. "I'm a director out in Hollywood."

"Oh? I thought you were Lucy's boyfriend. Seems to me that's what's important here."

"Max," Lucy chided, clearly not wanting him to cause trouble.

Lucas frowned at Max. "I'm both. I just thought you might have seen my movies—"

Max turned to Lucy. "We need to talk."

"But—" She glanced at her boyfriend.

"Go on," Lucas said. "He'll keep you busy while I'm working. Hell, he can take my place with your family for a little while." He dismissed Max, and his focus returned to his cell phone.

Either he wasn't smart enough to realize Max was a threat, or he just didn't care, because he strode off, heading for the yard exit.

"What the hell are you doing with a dickhead like that?" Max couldn't help but ask her.

Lucy spun around to face him, her cheeks flushed with embarrassment. "He's in the middle of a big deal that's stressful and—"

"Don't make excuses for him."

She folded her arms across her chest, and though she showed no cleavage, the movement pulled the silk material across her full breasts, revealing tight, perky nipples. Max's cock shot to attention, and he shifted his stance to alleviate the sudden discomfort.

She caught his gaze and frowned. "Quit staring at my breasts, you pervert." She followed that statement with a roll of her eyes.

He shook his head at her reaction. If he were at Paradis, the BDSM club he attended in Manhattan, he'd pull her over his knee and give her a good spanking. Another reason he'd stayed away from Lucy recently. In the years since his marriage, he'd discovered his tastes weren't always purely vanilla. But as he'd watched Lucy mature, he'd sensed she'd suit him fine. Outside the bedroom, she gave him hell, but his gut told him that once he showed her how good they could be together, she'd submit nicely in the bedroom. Hell, if he had Lucy, he wouldn't care about domination or submission. Those things had let him control something when the rest of his life felt out of control. All he really needed with Lucy was really good, hot sex.

He reached out and placed his hand beneath her chin, tipping her face until she met his gaze. "Admit it. You like the way I'm looking at you."

She blinked in stunned surprise because he was changing the game. They'd always sparred . . . and steered clear of the underlying sexual tension that surrounded them, which often led to arguing over nothing. Not this time. He intended to confront that sexual tension head on.

"Come with me." He grasped her wrist and tugged.

She resisted, then finally gave in, following him across the lawn and around the corner of the colonial-style house, where they could be alone. He stopped at a large cypress tree that probably predated construction and pulled her behind the trunk.

"Max, I don't think this is a good idea."

He spun her around until her back was against the trunk and stepped in close. Her delicious scent surrounded him, a mixture of peaches and something else. His gut twisted while his cock swelled even more.

For the first time, he wasn't fighting what he felt for her, what he needed.

"I think this is the very best idea."

Her cheeks flushed a healthy pink, her eyes bright with confusion. "I don't understand."

He reached up and sunk his hands into her hair, dislodging the staid updo she wouldn't be wearing if not for her asshole boyfriend, and tugged his fingers through the long strands.

"Max!"

She reached up to fix herself, but he caught her wrists in his hands and backed her farther into the tree, his body firmly nestled against her softness. His erection settled between her thighs, hot and hard, begging for relief and release. No way could she miss how much he wanted her.

She met his gaze, her eyes wide with surprise and darkening with desire.

"Answer my question, Lucy. What are you doing with that guy?"

"Oh my God. Lucas!" she said. Obviously she'd forgotten all about the man, and now she shifted in an attempt to get free.

Max held her firmly in place.

"I shouldn't be here with you," she said, but the heat in her eyes didn't match her words.

"You should definitely be here with me. So you can feel us, then take a good look at that so-called relationship you're in and do something about it."

Lucy heard his words and tried to fight her body's opposing response. Panicking, she tried once more to wriggle out of his grasp, but Max's strong, hard body held her in place.

His sandalwood scent enveloped her and softened places in her body she barely acknowledged these days. Her nipples were tight and hard, poking through her silk blouse, and her sex pulsed with unaccustomed need. This was *Max*. And yes, she'd had a crush on him for years, but that was a long time ago, and she'd been forced to accept that he didn't see her *that* way.

Hell, he'd married someone else when she was twenty-three and so available that she'd have done anything to make him her own. His engagement had been a blow, one that had hit her already-bruised heart harder than she ever could have imagined. She'd lost her parents and built stupid forever dreams around Max Savage. He may not have known, but when he'd married someone else, Lucy had been devastated.

She'd grasped on to another dream, being in charge of decor for the family clubs, and headed to California. Not only hadn't she come home for Max's wedding, but, on seeing the invitation, she'd decided to remain in LA for good. She'd suffered enough loss and pain to last a lifetime. With her brothers moving forward, finding good women to love, Lucy knew she wasn't needed here.

Losing Max—though she'd never really had him—had forced her to toughen up. She chose men she didn't have a chance of falling head over heels in love with, men whose loss wouldn't gut her. She had forced herself to return home for Max's wife's funeral, understanding all too well what grief and loss were like.

That was four long years ago. They'd since returned to their sibling-like bickering whenever they were together. Her last trip home, she'd actually wondered if the arguing was a way to cover sexual tension, but she'd pushed the idea deep down and far away, telling herself she was crazy. He'd never really given any indication he thought of her *that* way.

Until now.

When his chiseled, muscled body held her prisoner against the tree and her body thrummed with such intense need, she was seconds away from wriggling her hips and moving shamelessly against him. From grinding herself into his thick, hard erection and taking what she needed until she came—screaming—and the party guests surrounded them to find out what the ruckus was about.

She couldn't cross that line with Max. They shared a complicated relationship as it was, with a depth of emotion and caring she'd never felt for another man. And that made him dangerous to her mental and emotional well-being.

She gathered her strength and met his gaze. "What's going on, Max? You see me with another man, and you decide to get jealous all of a sudden?"

His dirty-blond hair fell over his forehead, and she curled her hands into fists, resisting the urge to brush it back. Heck, it wasn't just his hair she was dying to touch.

"Am I jealous?" He shrugged. "Only that you're here with him. I'm not particularly worried you're going to stay with him though."

The cords of his neck protruded, tight and tense, and she wasn't buying the attempt at nonchalance. "That's a cocky statement."

He let out a low, rumbling laugh she felt everywhere. "He doesn't appreciate you for who you are, princess."

"How would you know that?" she asked indignantly. Though a part of her knew he was right, Max was in no position to judge her or her choice in men.

"Let's begin with this." He slid a finger down her silk shirt, causing her already tight nipples to make their presence known even more. "While the soft material suits you fine, you like your clothes brighter, tighter, and showing more of that beautiful body."

He undid her blouse, button by tiny button, until she could breathe more freely and her cleavage was exposed. Her breath hitched, and she couldn't summon an argument, merely watched his big hands so close to her skin.

"You prefer a big piece of statement jewelry around your neck or letting that sexy tanned skin show. Mr. Uptight probably has his own requirements, though damned if I understand why he'd want to hide your light," he said as his roughened fingertips glided over her skin.

Her knees buckled, but Max's body weight supported her.

Still, she held on to rational thought. "Don't judge Lucas. He needs to project a certain image when he's approaching people to give money to his films."

"Then let him find a woman just like him. Not someone he needs to change. I wouldn't ask you to change for me." He cupped her neck in his hands, and a soft, needy moan escaped her lips.

"Max," she whispered.

"What?"

Don't do this. The words stuck in her throat because her body and a traitorous emotionally needy part of her wanted it. Wanted his mouth devouring hers, his talented hands gliding over her breasts, her nipples, and inside her sex. She desired him and had for years.

"Why now?" she asked in a feeble attempt to halt the inevitable.

"Because it's long past time." He brushed his thumb over her damp lips before covering her mouth with his.

She met him with a moan of acceptance. His lips were firm, moving with determination and a grace she wouldn't have expected, and his tongue glided back and forth, urging her to open and let him inside. One more swipe and she parted for him. He swept in, starting slow, learning his way, growing ever bolder.

Every lick, taste, and touch resonated inside her, her body alive and tingling in ways she'd never experienced before. His hands slid behind her neck, and his fingers thrust into her hair again. Her hair fell down her back, and he groaned, threaded his hands through, and tugged the strands, causing a sudden, delicious throbbing between her legs. A needy moan escaped from the back of her throat.

"You like that?" he asked, pulling harder on her hair.

She rocked her hips into his, the equivalent of a nod or a yes.

"Fuck." He tilted her head for better, deeper access and kissed her long and hard, a low groan of appreciation rumbling from deep in his chest.

He conquered her mouth, and she allowed him to take what he wanted, mutual desire flaring between them, the kiss now out of control. She'd given up the fight the minute his mouth had touched hers, and now she slid her hands through his silky hair and held on as he devoured her. Teeth clashed, tongues twined, and her breasts rubbed against his shirt, her aching nipples seeking what little relief she could find.

Every fantasy Lucy had had over the years didn't hold up to reality. This was so much better. No man had ever kissed her this way, as if he couldn't live without her taste, without *her*.

She was so lost in his taste and desire that she wasn't prepared when he broke the kiss, and she gasped for air. Somehow she'd been breathing through him, with him. He still held her up, more gently than before, his torso supporting her weight, his arms braced on either side of her head.

His eyes gleamed bright with desire and, if she wasn't mistaken, more than a hint of satisfaction . . . and that made her nervous.

"Now tell me, has anyone else made you feel like this?" he asked.

His words brought her back to reality, and horror set in. She'd succumbed to Max so easily, as if Lucas meant nothing to her at all. Which wasn't true.

She and Lucas had a comfortable relationship. He was someone to talk to, to have dinner with, and occasionally, when they were in the mood, sex was actually good. That was all she wanted. After all, if she didn't become emotionally invested, she couldn't be devastated when the relationship ended. And they all ended eventually.

"Is that what this was about, Max? Proving a point? That we have chemistry? Bravo. You proved you could seduce me if you wanted to." She braced her hands on his shoulders and shoved him away.

"This wasn't about some damned point. This was to show you what we could have. You weren't about to listen to words. I had to act."

"Well, you put me in an awful situation."

"I just want you to *think*. If you're honest, there's only one conclusion you can come to—give us a real chance."

She stared at him as if he'd lost his mind. Maybe she'd lost her hearing. "Are you crazy? Where were you years ago?" she asked, horror setting in when she realized what she'd admitted to.

Shaking, she turned away and ran for the house, adjusting her pantsuit as she made her way there. She was a mess, her hair tangled around her face, her lips swollen and clothes undone. She'd have to sneak inside if she really wanted to fix herself and hide the evidence of her betrayal. Isabelle wouldn't mind if Lucy used her things, so she'd head to the master bedroom and lock herself inside. Hopefully nobody would see her if she went in through the front and avoided the partygoers in the back.

She slipped into the main entrance and darted for the stairs, then enclosed herself in the master bath. Alone, she sighed and gripped the marble countertop hard. Max Savage had just kissed her. Hell, he'd ravaged her in broad daylight, and she'd let him. And he'd been the one to break the kiss, not her.

Lucy had never considered herself a cheater, so what had she been thinking? She shook her head, knowing the answer. She hadn't been. There'd been a time when she would have been ready for Max. When she'd still held on to fantasies of older, sexy Max Savage turning those amber eyes on her and claiming her as his own. Then he'd fallen in love and gotten married, shattering any foolish dreams of Max protecting her from the harsh outside world of loss.

Instead, he'd handed her more.

So she'd grown up and found safety in independence and distance. She'd graduated college, moved to California, helped decorate the family clubs her brother Gabe ran. Living on the West Coast, she could keep up with, and care about, Gabe and Decklan from afar. Protect herself and her heart . . . should something tragic happen to them like it had to her parents. Being isolated had also prepared her for the day when her brothers found their own families . . . and they had. She could love from a distance. It was safer.

Lucas was a safe choice. She knew her brothers didn't like him, but they didn't understand him either. He was busy and usually preoccupied with whatever film he was working on at any given time, which made him come off as abrupt and uncaring. But weren't her brothers busy too? Gabe ran a nightclub empire, and Decklan had been promoted to police detective . . . but their women took priority. For Lucy, it had taken a lot of pleading to get Lucas to come to New York with her for her brother's engagement, and he still hadn't committed to joining her in Eden for the wedding. Still, he was here now.

And he wouldn't approve of this messy version of herself. In Hollywood, appearances were important, and she told herself she didn't mind playing a role, dressing the way he preferred. Not the way her family was used to. As she smoothed her blouse with shaking hands, she realized how well Max knew what she liked, how he preferred the real Lucy Dare.

She bit down on her lower lip, reminding herself it didn't matter what Max liked. She and Lucas were compatible. And if she didn't see fireworks when Lucas kissed her, so what? They clicked. Neither gave the other a hard time if they had to work late or couldn't see each other for long stretches. Unlike her brothers, who barely let Amanda and Isabelle out of their sight whenever possible. And the way they looked at their women . . . Max had looked at her that way, she thought with a full-body shiver, right before his lips had descended on hers.

She trembled, her entire body still singing from that nearly public, sizzling-hot, tongue-tangling, soul-touching kiss. She still hadn't recovered from the emotional assault on her senses, nor had she begun to figure out how she felt about it. Well, she knew how her body felt—her blood ran hot, her skin still tingled, and the kiss kept replaying on an endless loop in her brain. She had to refrain from running her fingers over her still-sensitive lips.

In the course of ten short minutes, Max Savage had ripped away any shred of safety and sanity she'd possessed, leaving her raw and fragile. If she ever were to get involved with Max, she'd fall hard, and if she lost him, she didn't know if she'd find her way back from the pain.

Somehow she refreshed her makeup, a swipe of blush on her cheeks and gloss on her well-kissed lips. She worked on her hair next, but each pass of the brush led to instant recall of Max's fingers pulling at the long strands and the way her sex had pulsed in reaction. She didn't understand the tug of desire that action had evoked, but she knew she'd never experienced such intense longing before. Even now, her panties were still damp, her body aching and needy. In the end, she didn't put her hair back up, unable to replicate the updo she'd had before.

She made her way down the stairs and headed back outside, finding Lucas at their rental car, which he was using as his makeshift office. "Lucas."

He held up one finger, indicating she should wait, and continued his phone call.

She glanced into the bright blue sky. Her brother and Amanda had lucked out with the weather, she thought as Lucas droned on. Finally, he disconnected the call.

"Ready to leave?" he asked hopefully.

She shook her head and groaned. He really wasn't interested in her family, her life, or the things and people that mattered to her. But she wasn't ready to give up on him yet.

He sat in the back seat, car door open, facing outside into the sun, jotting down notes.

"Lucas? What are we doing?"

"Going back to the hotel, where I can work in comfort, I hope."

She bit the inside of her cheek. "I'm staying, Lucas. If you keep complaining about being here and sitting in the car doing work, I'd rather you just went back to LA." She folded her arms across her aching chest. "But if you care about me, you'll stay here and try to get to know my family." Her voice quivered along with her insides.

No matter what, she hadn't traveled out here planning to end her relationship. She hadn't even considered the reasons she should. But now they were flittering around the edges of her mind . . . and she blamed Max. Max, who still might mess up everything she had in LA. Because if Lucas chose to stay and try to make things work, she'd have to tell him about that kiss and face the consequences. If he didn't choose to stick around, well, he was stating he didn't care enough to bother. In which case, she had no reason to hurt him with the knowledge. If he even cared enough to *be* hurt.

She met his gaze and waited.

He narrowed his gaze. "I don't understand. I thought we complemented each other. No muss, no fuss, no hassle." He sounded genuinely confused about why she was suddenly questioning things.

Though she'd thought about their relationship in much the same stark terms, hearing him phrase things so blandly hurt. Didn't she want to mean more to someone than that? Damn Max for stirring up all these feelings and realizations.

"I thought that was enough for me, but coming here and seeing my family again, realizing how happy my brothers are . . . I'm not sure it is."

He glanced at her through his dark sunglasses. "Wait one minute. What happened to your hair?" he asked, narrowing his gaze as he obviously really looked at her for the first time.

She ran a hand down the long strands, no longer pinned back tight the way he preferred. "I—"

"And your blouse is unbuttoned." His jaw clenched. "You know I don't like you looking like . . . like a tramp."

She flinched. "Something happened . . . with Max." She swallowed hard and forced herself to continue despite the cruel sting of his words. "I was going to tell you. I didn't initiate it, but he kissed me. I'm sorry, but—"

Lucas rose and stood too close, anger vibrating off his body. "You didn't suddenly look at your brothers' relationships and decide that what we shared wasn't enough for you. Jesus Christ. You fucking kissed that guy, and now you're giving me an ultimatum you know damn well I won't accept."

"Lucas—"

She reached out for him, but he flung off her touch and attempt to calm him.

"It didn't mean anything," she assured him, even as her pounding heart and memories of Max's sexy mouth and hot body declared her words a lie. But she couldn't let inconvenient feelings mess up her well-ordered life. She wanted the safe and easy relationship she and Lucas shared.

"I took precious time off from work and traveled all the way out here, and you cheated on me like a common whore." He slammed the back door hard.

She jumped at the sound, shocked at his crude words. "It wasn't like that."

"Don't fucking talk to her like that." Max stepped between them while Lucy stood stunned. Lucas's words had hit too close to home, and he'd never spoken to her like that before.

Lucas glared at Max, clearly assessing his angry competition. Max boxed for sport and fitness. Lucas didn't. From the tight clench of Max's fists to the muscles bulging in his forearms, he was damned close to taking a swing.

"I don't have time for this bullshit or for you," Lucas finally muttered. He stalked past her, brushing his shoulder against hers as he headed for the driver's seat.

"Touch her again and you'll be picking your teeth off the floor one by one," Max muttered.

"Screw you." Lucas closed himself inside the Lincoln Town Car, started the engine, floored the gas, and drove away without looking back.

Lucy closed her eyes, hating how things had turned out between them. She'd rather have ended things the right way, but Max had forced the issue.

And she hadn't pushed him away.

Get *Dare to Seduce* now at your
local bookstore or buy online!

ABOUT THE AUTHOR

Carly Phillips is the *New York Times* and *USA Today* bestselling author of more than fifty sexy contemporary romance novels featuring hot men, strong women, and the emotionally compelling stories her readers have come to expect and love. Carly's career spans over a decade and a half with various New York publishing houses, and she is now an indie author who runs her own business and loves every exciting minute of her publishing journey. Carly is happily married to her college sweetheart and is the mother of two nearly adult daughters and three crazy dogs (two wheaten terriers and one mutant Havanese) who star on her Facebook fan page and website. Carly loves social media and is always around to interact with her readers. You can find out more about Carly at www.carlyphillips.com.

Carly's Booklist by Series

Dare to Love Series
Book 1: *Dare to Love* (Ian & Riley)
Book 2: *Dare to Desire*
(Alex & Madison)
Book 3: *Dare to Touch*
(Olivia & Dylan)
Book 4: *Dare to Hold* (Scott & Meg)
Book 5: *Dare to Rock* (Avery & Grey)
Book 6: *Dare to Take* (Tyler & Ella)

NY Dares Series
Book 1: *Dare to Surrender*
(Gabe & Isabelle)
Book 2: *Dare to Submit*
(Decklan & Amanda)
Book 3: *Dare to Seduce*
(Max & Lucy)

*The NY Dares books are
more erotic/hotter books.

Serendipity Series
Serendipity
Destiny
Karma

Serendipity's Finest Series
Perfect Fit
Perfect Fling
Perfect Together

Serendipity Novellas
Fated
Hot Summer Nights
(Perfect Stranger)

Bachelor Blog Series
Kiss Me If You Can
Love Me If You Dare

Lucky Series
Lucky Charm
Lucky Streak
Lucky Break

Ty and Hunter Series
Cross My Heart
Sealed with a Kiss

Hot Zone Series
Hot Stuff
Hot Number
Hot Item
Hot Property

Costas Sisters Series
Summer Lovin'
Under the Boardwalk

Chandler Brothers Series
The Bachelor
The Playboy
The Heartbreaker

Stand-Alone Titles
Brazen
Seduce Me
Secret Fantasy
The Right Choice
Suddenly Love
Perfect Partners
Unexpected Chances
Worthy of Love

Keep up with Carly and her upcoming books:

Website:
www.carlyphillips.com

Sign up for blog and website updates:
www.carlyphillips.com/category/blog/

Sign up for Carly's newsletter:
www.carlyphillips.com/newsletter-sign-up

Carly on Facebook:
www.facebook.com/CarlyPhillipsFanPage

Carly on Twitter:
www.twitter.com/carlyphillips

Hang out at Carly's Corner—hot guys & giveaways!
smarturl.it/CarlysCornerFB